# GHOST TOWN

There wasn't supposed to be anyone here.

Cinch drew his pistol, smoothly and quickly, pointing it in the general direction of the shadows eight meters ahead of him. "Wouldn't be a good idea to move," he called out. "Unless you do it real slow."

He might feel a little silly if a deer or a monkey bolted from the shade. But that was better than feeling a little dead if it were one of the people who'd racked up this village.

Somebody moved slowly into the sunshine.

The ranger blinked.

A woman with a gun stood there staring at Cinch, a black-haired, black-eyed woman with a tan like good holster leather.

She was naked.

*Other AvoNova Books by*
**Steve Perry**

STELLAR RANGER

# STELLAR RANGER

## LONE ★ STAR

## STEVE PERRY

AVON BOOKS • NEW YORK

STELLAR RANGER: LONE STAR is an original publication of Avon
Books. This work has never before appeared in book form. This work is
a novel. Any similarity to actual persons or events is purely coincidental.

AVON BOOKS
A division of
The Hearst Corporation
1350 Avenue of the Americas
New York, New York 10019

First AvoNova Printing: January 1995

AVONOVA TRADEMARK REG. U.S. PAT. OFF. AND IN OTHER COUNTRIES, MARCA
REGISTRADA, HECHO EN U.S.A.

Printed in the U.S.A.

RA   10   9   8   7   6   5   4   3   2   1

This book is for Dianne;
And also for the Jeans:
Jeanne Arbow, Jean Naggar,
Jeanie Dickens, and Jean Auel.

# ACKNOWLEDGMENTS

Help this time came from the usual crew: add to them Bill Fawcett for the work; Vince Kohler, for some fine times at the TriCounty Gun Club; Al Dacascos, the latest in a long line of expert martial arts instructors. And, oh, yeah, William "Kill 'em all" Dietz—this one ought to make you happy, Bill.

The standard disclaimer applies, the one where the writer says if there are mistakes, it's his fault because he screwed up the input. (Although just once I'd like to see somebody say, "Yeah, and if there are mistakes, it's *their* fault because I wrote it just like they told me." But I ain't gonna say that, thank you.)

And I would be remiss if I didn't thank a couple of people who are no longer with us: Edgar Rice Burroughs, who figured out that writing was easier than selling pencil sharpeners; and, finally, Robert E. Howard, whose strapping creation has given a lot of writers a hand over the years and who has certainly been very good to me. Thanks, folks.

"O! that estates, degrees and offices
Were not deriv'd corruptly, and that clear honor
Were purchas'd by the merit of the wearer."

William Shakespeare
*The Merchant of Venice*


"He laughs best who laughs last."

Sir John Vanbrugh
*The Country House*

# chapter 1

If you believed in such things, this would be a ghost town.

The bodies had been removed, and the villagers who had survived the attack evacuated, so the place was now home only to the braver animals of the wood, the ones who ventured in after the humans were gone. It could have been any of a thousand small towns carved into the fringes of a dense rain forest on any one of a dozen jungle worlds he had visited before.

Rudyard "Cinch" Carston stood in front of a shattered permaplast wall, the watery-pale blue of the material sending off heat waves that smelled like burned circuits beneath the heavy touch of Mtizito's tropical sun. A line of splintered holes, each as big around as his middle finger, had been stitched across the wall; the high-velocity slugs, probably from a plasma rifle on full auto, had punched through. It wouldn't have been much cover: anybody standing on the other side of the wall would have been cut down unless they'd been wearing military-grade body armor.

Cinch moved away from the ruined wall. Probably hadn't been a whole lot of military-grade body armor available to the villagers when they were attacked.

He pulled his hat off, a wide-brimmed, low-crowned

plantation-style affair favored by the locals, and wiped at his forehead with the sweatband around his right wrist. Along with the hat and band, he wore tropical weight polyprop shorts and a shirt, both khaki-colored, sweat-socks, and lightweight hiking boots. He had his antique Smith strapped around his waist, the pinchnose holster holding the pistol firmly but offering quick accessibility to the weapon. He also had a com, small flatscreen, a bugbuster, and a carry pouch crowed to his belt. He put the hat back on. With these clothes and his own fairly deep tan, he should be able to pass for a native of Mtizito, at least to a local eye. His badge and ID, showing him to be a Stellar Ranger, were tucked out of sight in the pouch.

He walked through the remains of the village. It was just past noon and the heat lay on the place like a wet sheet. Insects buzzed him, but kept their distance, repelled by the electronic device he carried.

Somebody had used a pyrotube on this house, the permaplast was puddled in frizzy globs where it had melted from the intense heat. The next house—no, it had been a market of some kind—had felt the hammer of an explosive, the walls knocked flat on two sides, the other two leaning askance. Slapflex cord, maybe, or D6. The characteristic smell of D6, like a mound of crushed ants, would have long since dissipated. If he'd brought a sniffer, he could have picked up enough stray molecules even two weeks after the event to tell what kind of bomb it had been, but that didn't really matter. Forensic science sometimes got into navel-picking and lost sight of the goal. What kind of bomb had blown this building down wasn't nearly so important as who had launched it, and why.

Cinch circled the block, looking at the signs of destruction. He shook his head. Whoever had done this had spent a lot of ordnance on it and not very wisely. Sure, it was burned or blasted all to hell and gone, but it could have been leveled a whole lot easier and cheaper by anybody with any military experience at all. This place looked as if it had been attacked by a bunch of psychotic children who'd been given dangerous toys and told to go play.

He rounded a corner. A particularly large flying insect bounced off his head, going too fast for the bugbuster to stop its flight. Cinch swatted at the thing, a half second too late. It was already gone by the time his hand fanned hot air into his eyes. It distracted him for a moment, so that the movement from the hard shadow of a relatively undamaged building just ahead almost escaped him.

Almost escaped him, but not quite.

There wasn't supposed to be anybody here; the governor had told him the village was off-limits.

Cinch drew his pistol, smoothly and quickly, and brought it up to a two-hand isosceles hold, pointing in the general direction of the shadows eight meters ahead of him. His grandfather had given him the gun, a compressed gas slugthrower that had been an antique when the old man got it. The weapon held six lead bullets, the rounds shaped and trimmed so they would starfish on impact even at the pistol's low velocity. There were three ways to aim the pistol: a laser sight, a red dot, and a notch-and-post. Cinch was good enough at this range to point-shoot without using any of the sights and hit a hand-sized spot all day long. Not as good as a rifle or a splatgun, the pistol would stop an unprotected man nine times out of ten with a single shot to the body.

"Wouldn't be a good idea to move," he called out. "Unless you do it real slow."

He might feel a little silly if a deer or a monkey bolted from the shade, but that was better than feeling a little dead if it were one of the people who'd racked up this village.

Somebody moved slowly into the sunshine.

The ranger blinked.

A woman stood there staring at Cinch, a black-haired, black-eyed woman with a tan like good holster leather.

She was naked.

Well, except for some narrow stripes of bright red and blue paint on her face and body—and the plasma rifle she had pointed at the ranger's belly—she was naked. Her smile showed a lot of good teeth and looked genuinely happy, but the expression was a little on the wolfish side for Cinch's taste. There was nothing wrong with the rest of her, though, nothing at all.

They stood there for maybe three seconds, neither of them moving. Then Cinch lowered his pistol so that it pointed at the ground by his feet. If she had wanted to kill him, he'd already be dead; she could have fired from cover before he ever saw her.

She also lowered her weapon so that it pointed at the ground. It would be easy enough to snap it up if he tried to use his pistol and she had to know her gun would do a lot more damage than his.

Something made a noise behind him. Despite the naked woman with the rifle in front of him, Cinch flicked a look to see what might be sneaking up on him.

This time, it *was* a monkey, a small gray-skinned creature that bounded across the road on all fours, heading for the safety of the jungle that lapped at the edge of the village.

By the time he looked back for his nude adversary, she was gone.

He went to look for her, but there wasn't any sign he could spot.

He grinned as he holstered his pistol. Well. That was a hell of a way to start the day. A Mexican standoff with a beautiful naked woman. In all his years of smuggling and then rangering, he couldn't say that had ever happened to him before—

A bullet smashed through the wall next to his head; he heard it hit before the sound of the weapon that threw it arrived.

Cinch dived, rolled, and came up behind the corner of

the building, what had once been a grain storehouse. He half crawled, half ran along the wall away from the sound of the shot, his pistol out and in his hand again without conscious thought of having drawn it. It wasn't the woman shooting at him, he knew. She couldn't have gotten that far away in such a short time, and the shot had echoed from a distance, maybe 150 meters, if he had to guess. Were they stalking him or had they been looking for her? Was the shooter the woman's confederate?

*Later, Cinch, worry about that later.* First and most important, he had to dodge the shooter. Manage that, and he could worry about the rest.

He moved, senses alert. He hadn't thought to bring his wolf ears or spookeyes. The ears probably wouldn't do much good with all the masking jungle noises he could hear without them, and it would have to be a hell of a lot darker before the spookeyes would drop the flare shutters and let him see anything.

But after ten minutes of waiting, Cinch was pretty sure whoever had taken the shot at him was gone. He circled the village twice more in the next half hour—even when it had been whole, no more than three or four thousand people had lived here—without finding anything but a couple of monkeys and the local equivalent of a pig rooting for mushrooms in a long-rotted log.

No shooter.

No naked woman, either.

Too bad.

The man who led the charge was tall, two meters easy, with red hair and a beard that gave him a piratical look. He wore raggy shorts that had seen better days or years, no shirt or shoes. His skin seemed burnished red rather than tan, and he waved a field-grade pulse rifle back and forth, firing quarter-second bursts of hard purple light from the hip. He had a triple-stack capacitor pack strapped around his waist. He also had plenty of muscle; it clung like ship

hawsers to his frame, flexing and bulging as he ran. He
looked like a demented bodybuilder.

Somebody screamed.

Behind the red giant came a dozen other bandits,
dressed in raggy clothes, some with shirts, some without,
but all using pulse or plasma rifles new enough so they
didn't show any signs of wear, no annealing at the barrel
crown, no static burns on the actions. They dressed like
riffraff but each carried several thousand cees worth of
hardware, counting the capacitor packs, or in the case of
the plasma weapons, spare plates of ammo hung on belts
or bandoliers.

Somebody ran past, a short man, heading away at an angle. Red Beard turned and flashed him. At three meters,
the pulse rifle's beam hit and splashed, a corona of laven-
der that looked almost pretty. Radiation that evaporated
hair, ate skin and muscle, and charred bone couldn't really
be called pretty, though, not unless you could divorce it
from the effect. The dead man—and there was no doubt of
that—had been cooked in his own juices. Sometimes people hit with pulse beams exploded, they boiled so fast.

A bomb went off in the background, shaking the
ground. The boom was oddly muted but the concussive
wave hit and the scene went dark . . .

Even sitting in a plush room weeks after it happened,
Cinch could almost feel the fury of the attack. The
holoproj image stayed dark and, after a moment, the air
cleared as the recording shut off.

"This was from a cam mounted at an intersection," the
governor said. "The settlers were thinking of putting a
traffic signal in, the number of vehicles in town had been
increasing. Four or five hundred carts, maybe." He shook
his head. "I've seen this a dozen times and it still churns
my guts every time."

Cinch nodded.

"The red-haired man is Munga Vita," the governor said.

"He's the leader of one of the three main militant native factions."

The ranger nodded again. The speaker, Yogen Groiss Lavan, was a beefy man a few years older than Cinch, maybe sixty, nearing middle age. He had white hair and a white beard, both trimmed short, and wore a flowing robe of muted silver glowsilk that Cinch guessed cost three thousand cees; under the robe were what looked to be handmade ostrich-skin slippers. According to Cinch's background check on the way in-planet, Lavan had been middle-class before he decided to run for political office. As governor of Kivu, the most populated state on the Northern Continent, he had considerable control over the two million or so "new" settlers who had arrived or been born in the last sixty years. Since this was where all the people were, being governor effectively made him the most powerful man on the planet. Cinch had what the ranger comp could deliver on the world, but he wanted to get the view from the top.

"Something to drink?"

"The local beer any good?"

"The dark brew is passable."

"A beer, then."

Lavan waved his hand over an intercom. "Bring our guest a Negrito. And a fizzer for me."

It took maybe thirty seconds for the drinks to arrive, brought by a short and pretty woman with shocked blue hair and breasts too large to be hidden under her loose robe, also of glowsilks, only hers were a deep crimson. Lavan must pay his staff well.

The beer, in a tall pilsner glass with a froster built into the base, was excellent. He said as much to Lavan.

"We grow pretty good hops and grain here and make several good beers—when the savages aren't blowing up the breweries."

Cinch took another sip of the beer. "So, tell me how this came to be."

Lavan laughed. "It would take weeks to lay out the long version."

"The short course will do."

"Okay." He leaned back in his chair, a custom orthopedia that had to be made offworld. The seat hummed and adjusted itself to his contours. "Mtizito was settled originally during the First Wave. Hawking ships. Everything went fine at first, then about sixty years after the colony was established, some dinjab in a lab screwed up. A mutant biological escaped, right in the middle of Chumvi, the old capital city fifty klicks north of here. Town was established on a wide salt flat that ran all the way to the ocean, didn't require any forest clearing and whatnot to get construction up in a hurry.

"Well. The bug was some kind of *E. coli*. It started what was called the Tumbo la Kuhara, the Diarrhea Plague. There were about a million people onplanet at the time and it killed three-quarters of them within a year. The survivors were those who stayed out in the bush, mostly, river rats, outbackers, jungle jammers. Lots of antisocial types, crazies, the usual frontier riffraff."

Cinch sipped at the dark beer.

"The people left went native. Had various cults and cliques and if they didn't degenerate to the spear-chucking category, they came close. They turned paranoid, insular, bloodthirsty. Civilization more or less faded and the jungle took over big chunks of what had been here.

"So, cut to eighty years later. More settlers start to show up, the Salinas Drive making it a lot quicker and easier. They started putting the chaos here in order. It wasn't easy then—that was in my grandfather's time—records had been destroyed, the natives were quick to shoot first and not ask any questions if you stepped on their local taboo. Since, we've been slowly bringing order to the world, at least to the Elbow—"

"Elbow?"

Lavan smiled. "That's what the name of the continent

means. If nothing else, the FW were colorful in their names."

"Sorry. Go ahead."

Lavan shrugged and sipped at his drink. Cinch didn't know what a fizzy was, exactly, but it didn't look or smell alcoholic.

"Not much else to tell in the short version. The descendants of the FW are still mostly savages. Those who wanted to take advantage of civilization have done so; the rest of them grub around in the jungles like animals and want nothing to do with us. The three dissident groups that have risen to prominence are the most hard-line. They basically want everybody who arrived after the FW to pull up stakes and leave."

Lavan laughed again. "They're not very bright out there in the bush. We've established laws to protect them and their rights, to help them mainstream, but they don't appreciate it. They are vicious, violent, and apt to shoot you as look at you, smiling all the while."

Cinch finished his beer, set the glass down on the table in front of his chair. "And you want the rangers to fix this?"

The man liked to laugh. "No, no, certainly not. We've been working on it for eighty years and we haven't made a big dent in their attitude. But if you can help us find and capture the leaders of the most vicious factions, we can force them to listen to reason. So far, we haven't been able to get close enough. By the time our jump troops arrive at one of these massacres"—he waved at the air where the holoproj had been—"the murderers always seem to have vanished. They strike and run and we can't get a line on where they've gone. All we want you to do is help us find them. We'll do the rest."

"Well. I'll see what I can do."

The governor stood. "I'd like to visit longer but I have pressing matters of state that must be attended to." He held his palm out and down in a peace gesture.

Cinch stood and mimicked the move.

"You'll have total cooperation from our people," Lavan said. "Transportation, supplies, infonet access, whatever you need. You saw what they did to that village—it has to stop. We need your help, M. Carston, and we're willing to do anything to bring peace to our planet."

Cinch left the governor's office. The young woman who'd brought them drinks was in the anteroom and she smiled brightly at him as he departed.

As he walked down the marble steps of the building into the tropical sunshine, he smiled to himself. All he had to do was go out into the jungle, locate and capture the leaders of three rebel factions, and bring them in. No problem, right? One ranger, one planet?

Yeah. Right.

# chapter 2

Governor Lavan pretended to ignore the ranger as he left. The man didn't seem to be particularly impressive, which was about what Lavan had expected. Mtizito wasn't a major player out here in its quiet stillvackness, hardly a place or a situation to warrant sending your best man.

The governor fiddled with a flatscreen, staring at the readout but not really seeing it. On the one hand, this was exactly as he had hoped for—that the rangers would send a second-stringer to poke around in the native problem and he wouldn't be any trouble. A little flash and dazzle, some artful misdirection, and the doob would wind up chasing phantoms—and his own tail. Ten years as governor had given Lavan more than a little skill in blowing smoke, it was the second thing a successful politician learned—right after ass-covering.

On the other hand, he was a little disappointed, in a perverse kind of way. The Stellar Rangers had a reputation: they were supposed to be able to chew steel plates, spit needles, and pin a crook to a wall a parsec away. Carston looked like a flitter in need of an overhaul. He was worn around the edges and he didn't seem all that bright. Probably in his younger days he'd been a fast gun and fairly quick on his feet, but he was a bit long in the tooth to still be out in the field. Not that he was old, probably ten years younger than Lavan and that wasn't even middle age; still, a sharper man would have been bumped up into management by now. It was to Lavan's advantage, of course, and as he had expected, but still, it was one more bit of mythology punctured and deflated.

So much for the much-heralded Stellar Rangers.

"Governor, you've got a com from Mayor Uma, channel six."

Lavan smiled at the young woman in the crimson glowsilks. Pakita was a sub-secretary, hired not for her business acumen but for her physical attributes and certain ... *other* talents she possessed. Her responsibilities consisted mainly of screening his communications—and providing enjoyable diversions, often while he spoke on-com to one boring functionary or another. She was a native, part of the governor's effort to help the underclass, and doubtless the various mayors, councilfolk, and business types would be surprised to see what Pakita was sometimes doing just below camera frame as the governor spoke to them. Of course, seeing her busy mouth and hands would explain why he smiled so much as he talked ...

Lavan found he was interested in having those particular ministrations applied, and he motioned for Pakita to follow him into his inner office.

She gave him a sly smile.

Lavan sat in his orthopedia, reset the angle of the chair, and waved the office com to life.

"Ah, Mayor Uma. How are you?"

The mayor's face shimmered as the holoproj flashed to life, giving Lavan an image of the man from mid-chest up. Which was also all the mayor would see of Lavan at his office in Kanisa City.

"Fine, Governor, fine. Yourself?"

"Oh, I'm—ah—feeling ... terrific right at the moment."

He smiled. *That* was sure the truth. Unseen by the mayor, he put his hand down and touched Pakita's head. Yes. Terrific. Everything was coming along perfectly.

Cinch walked along the busy street toward the house he'd rented, getting a feel for the city. Called Kiwanda, the place had the look and smell of many frontier metroplexes: there was a fossil fuel tang to the air from factories on the edges of town; an energetic hustle by pedestrians and vehicular traffic, this latter a blend of wheeled electric carts, GE and repellor-lifted flitters, vans, trucks, bicycles, fuel-cell motorcycles, and trikes. Everybody was always in a hurry on new worlds, busy, money to be made, places to go, things to do.

Cinch smiled as he waited with the other foot traffic at an intersection for a go-ahead signal. A massive twelve-wheeled electric van ignored the stop signal and nearly flattened an enclosed trike that putt-putted to a tire-burning halt on the plastcrete. The little three-wheeler's driver, a short and stout woman, leaned out and treated the rear of the offending van to a string of artfully constructed curses. She called the man's ancestry into question, indicating that, in her opinion, he had relatives far down the evolutionary scale—dogs, rats, snakes, and even mildew; more, according to the tricyclist, the driver of the offending van had enjoyed sexual relations with most, if not all, of his immediate family, including his sister, brother, and mother.

Cinch grinned wider. At least she wasn't shooting. He saw a carbine mounted across the rear of the trike's interior. While there weren't an awful lot of people walking around armed, there were some. Local laws allowed that, as they did on many frontier worlds. In a lot of places, there were still animals big enough to be dangerous to humans, as well as predators of their own species, and if you were a hundred klicks away from the nearest peace officer, you had to take care of your own problems. Here in the biggest city on the continent, you weren't as apt to run into man-eating cats or reptiles as you would be in the bush, so a lot of people apparently felt safe.

When it looked as if he could make it across the six lanes without being flattened by a truck, Cinch hurried to do so.

No skyscrapers here yet, at least not compared to what were considered such on a civilized world like Terra or Wu. There were a few buildings that might run fifteen, twenty stories, but as long as there was plenty of space to spread out, why go up? On Wu, if you had money to play with, you built yourself a house that had a tiny footprint but might climb twenty floors high. Land was dear, there was a lot more water than firma, and with two billion people on the Nine Isles, bonsai was a major hobby. Here, you could spread out on hectacres and not worry about your neighbors peeping in your windows—if you *had* any neighbors between you and the horizon. Cinch preferred that to living like ants in nest.

The house he had rented was really more of a cabin, but even here in the city, it sat on a lot big enough so there was a hundred meters between it and the next rental unit. It had fruit trees, tropical bushes covered with red or blue or yellow flowers, and a lawn of bright green grass that was either mowed or engineered to stay short. There were worlds on which his cabin, cheaply had here, would be considered a vacation paradise.

As he walked, the sky began to thicken, a rapid scud of wet-looking clouds that quickly smeared the sunlight to a diffused gray. A rumble of thunder told him the rain wasn't far off. Electrical storms were frequent on jungle worlds, the hotter, the heavier. His background research had spoken of the *wembemvua* here on Mtizito, the local cyclones or hurricanes. The name meant "razor rains," and according to his biblog, the worst of these would stomp ashore with winds topping 350 kph.

That was a stiff breeze on any planet where men could

live. At three hundred and some-odd klicks an hour, a broken tree branch could punch a hole right through you.

Lightning strobed, bright under the darkening sky, and the thunder growled closer and louder. Rain coming and fast. Cinch hadn't brought a hoop film or umbrella with him and he hurried to get to his cabin before the storm dropped its cargo.

He almost made it. He was only fifty meters from the cabin's door when the rain started. The gravity was almost TS, maybe a hair less, and the first scattered drops were fat and heavy. They spattered like tiny water balloons when they hit. Within five seconds, however, the sky opened up as if someone had turned a shower tap on full blast. Even if he ran as fast as he could, there was no way Cinch was going to avoid getting soaked. He mentally shrugged and kept his pace at a walk.

By the time he reached the cabin and the small roofed porch, the air had gone such a monochromatic gray he couldn't see more than a few meters into the afternoon. The cabin vibrated with the sound as the rain hammered it, driven aslant by hard gusts of wind.

Cinch grinned, water running down his face despite the planter's hat he still wore. His equipment was all supposedly waterproof, his pistol stainless steel and plastic, no damage. Still, he'd better carry his hoop film from now on if he wanted to stay dry. An umbrella wouldn't be much good the way this stuff was blowing every which way.

He smiled at himself. *Must be getting old, Carston. To be worrying about umbrellas and hoop film. Next thing you know, you'll be talking to the retirement people about the benefits of your pension. Then you'll start boring the ears off of everybody you meet, telling them about your aches and pains. Just another old fart ranger talking about the glory days, back when rangers were real men and not just button pushers sitting in a nice dry office somewhere . . .*

He shook the water off his hat, took off his boots and

socks, and put his keycard into the door's lock reader. The door clicked and started to open when a bolt of lightning struck something nearby. The boom that followed was simultaneous and loud enough to rattle the windows and vibrate deep in Cinch's chest. Close.

The side-hinged door swung outward maybe three centimeters, stopped, and the green diode on the lock blinked out.

Cinch put his boots down. Well. The power must have been disrupted by the lightning. That happened a lot during electrical storms on worlds where they still used aboveground transformer boxes. There must be a manual release lever somewhere, yeah, there it was—

But as Cinch reached for the lever, set flush in the jamb facing him, he stopped. Even with the power out in the cabin, he could see the thin black carbon wound-filament wire connected to the door's inside handle. A wire that was taut and connected at the other end to something in the darkness that he *couldn't* see.

Uh oh.

Damn.

# chapter 3

The easiest thing would have been for Cinch to leave his rented cabin and walk to the nearest dry spot to call the local police. They'd send somebody from the bomb unit, assuming they had such things on this planet, and he could park himself across the street and watch the experts risk their necks—what they got paid for, right? If the other end of that string was in fact connected to an explosive device, that was probably the wisest course of action. Then again, the trap might not be attached to a bomb. Could be a gun. Or a bucket of water. Although he didn't know anybody on this world well enough for them to be springing practical jokes on him, he had to allow for the possibility.

As the rain pod blew through, slacking off on both wind and water, he considered his options. Bomb, gun, or a shower of confetti, whatever, he *was* a Stellar Ranger, and it wasn't seemly that he should be running to the local police to take care of his problems.

No, he'd tend to this himself.

Carefully, very carefully, he pulled the door shut. Nothing happened, at least nothing particularly explosive.

Since he was already wet, Cinch ambled out into the dwindling rain and circled around to the back of the cabin. Halfway there, the power came back on—it was dark enough so an outside light with a sensor kicked on in the overcast. The front door apparently didn't finish the cycle but reset itself—there wasn't an explosion or the sound of a shot and he couldn't hear it snick closed from where he was. Damn. He should have thought of that, should have jammed the door so it couldn't move. Not very sharp, ranger.

The back door didn't have a keyed or coded lock, just a simple spring-latch bolt operated from the inside. You could exit via the door but, unless somebody left it propped open, you couldn't normally enter that way— there wasn't a handle on the outside. Cinch pulled his pocketknife from his pouch. One of the blades was a thin strip of flexible surgical steel about six centimeters long. It took about forty seconds to snap the latch back and ease the door open a hair. If he stayed here, he'd have to do something about that.

He wasn't too worried about another trap, given that nobody ought to expect anybody to enter the cabin thus, but he was real careful just the same.

As far as he could tell, there wasn't any kind of backup device connected to the rear door.

Cinch eased the door open wider. The room lights went on as he stuck his arm inside, triggering the motion sensor. The cabin's interior was basically one big room, save for a small fresher off one end and a kitchenette on the other. There was a large hardgel-pad bed, a couch and two chairs, a table with a computer terminal and holoproj on it, a closet with a hanging rack in it, no door. Unless somebody was hiding in the fresher, he was alone.

On a chair propped in front of the front entrance was what appeared to be a rifle or shotgun, aimed so anybody coming in that way would find himself looking right down the barrel. Cinch was willing to bet big money at bigger odds that had he opened the door fully, the cord connection it to the weapon would have set the sucker off. At that range, he would have had to move faster than a hot Salinas

Drive to get out of the way before whatever the gun spit hit him. Even so, he felt better. A gun was easier to deal with than a bomb.

He pulled his pistol, gripped it in his right hand, and moved toward the fresher. His clothes and lockbox looked untouched, but he would have to see about that after he made sure the cabin was safe.

He shoved the fresher door open with his left hand, pistol held ready. Stood there in the puddle from his dripping clothes, prepared for trouble.

Nobody home.

The bidet sat quietly alone, the shower stall was empty, the tiny window too small to allow exit unless you were the size of a house cat, and it was closed and latched anyhow.

He made a circuit of the room, poking and prodding, looking for any other little surprises, but found none. They had come and gone, whoever they were.

When he was pretty sure the floor wasn't going to open up and swallow him or the walls weren't about to explode, he went to check the trap.

It was set to shoot whoever came through the door, all right. The wire ran through a pulley hook, looped around the back of the chair so that a tug would pull the trigger.

He went to his lockbox and fingerprinted it open. The computer inset into the box did not show any unauthorized attempts to break into it. Anybody who expected people to show up and find a dead ranger would probably not be so dumb as to leave obvious physical evidence; still, he dug through his gear and found his print sprayer. He pulled a pair of surgical gloves out, slipped them on, and went back to examine the trap. He unhooked the wire and looked at the weapon, then dusted it with the fine fluoropowder. He lit the UV lamp in the sprayer's base and went over the weapon.

It was clean.

Well. It never hurt to look.

He picked up the weapon and looked at it carefully. It was mostly plastic and spuncarb, a bolt action, with a plug covering a gas-fill valve in the buttstock. Safety off and ready to fire, the load diode showed one round in the chamber. Cinch opened the bolt, slowly, and pulled it back, easing the round from the breech. He plucked the projectile out and looked at it. The cartridge was some kind of chemical dart, a small clear reservoir full of blue-green fluid attached to a sharp steel hypodermic point with an inertial piston behind the chem to squirt the stuff through the needle when it hit a target. Pretty standard stuff.

Cinch moved to his lockbox and pulled his chemical analyzer out and put it online. He unscrewed the rear of the hypo and carefully pressed the rear of the piston with a light pen so that a couple of drops of the bluish chem fell into the jar of the analyzer's inert medium. He swirled the solution around and stuck it into the machine.

*Let's see how they wanted me to die.*

The test didn't take long. The holoprojic read spiked and valleyed, and gave him a generic name he recognized: Sleepstat. You want a printout with that? the machine queried.

My, my. It *wasn't* a fatal poison, just a knockout chem, good for maybe a half-hour nap and a bad hangover when you woke up.

Cinch shook his head. Somebody had set a trap for him and they wanted him out, but not dead. Maybe they had planned to come and collect him after it worked, which meant they had probably been watching him when he arrived. Must have ruined their whole day, first the rain, then him spotting the setup.

He could go out and make a pass looking for them, but he suspected that would be a waste of his time. If they had seen him come in and not get hit, likely they figured he would try to find them.

Cinch looked at the dart, twirled it in his fingers. Who

wanted to play games like this with him? Why? He hadn't
been here long enough to piss anybody off, had he?
Wouldn't it be easier just to knock on the damned door
and talk to him face-to-face? Yeah, you'd think so—unless
they had some reason that idea didn't appeal to them. Like
maybe they thought he might want to throw them in jail.

Hmm. Very interesting.

Lavan was eating a quarter kilo of very good pork,
baked and coated with sweet *iniya* glaze, when his personal com cheeped on his private opchan.

"Yes?"

"It's me," came the voice. Even on a supposedly leak-
proof and secure operations channel, Lavan's people never
used uncoded names, his, theirs, or anybody else's.

"So?"

"The subject went back to his place. Started to go inside, changed his mind, went around back, shimmed the
door, and went in that way."

"Why?"

"Dunno; no reason I could see. Doesn't make any sense
to me. Maybe he's paranoid."

"Where is he now?"

"Still in there. Alone. Quiet."

"Good. Maintain your surveillance. If he coughs, I want
to know the decibel level and the volume of air in it."

"Gotcha."

Lavan frowned at the com. The glaze on the pork
seemed too sweet all of a moment. The ranger shouldn't
be any problem, but when people did things they weren't
supposed to do, it bothered him. He didn't like surprises.
He didn't like them at all.

Cinch thought about using the room's terminal to access
the local infonet but decided that if somebody had physically entered the room, they could tap an unshielded 'cast
a lot easier. He pulled his own flatscreen, dialed up a

coded signal, and logged into the net. Not that what he wanted was particularly secret—maps, history, odds and ends that were perfectly innocuous in themselves. But he didn't want anybody knowing what he wanted; they knew that, they might be able to figure out why, and at this stage of the investigation, he would prefer to keep that to himself.

As he began to download the files, Cinch remembered his most recent prior assignment. On Roget, he had wound up chasing a rich man with a bunch of secrets and a lot of what seemed obvious on the surface turned out to be otherwise in the end. He should have learned by now after all his years of rangering not to assume too much before he had the facts laid out cold. This native problem might not be quite so simple as it appeared, either.

Well. He had the governor's version of the story. Now it was time to find out what the other side had to say.

He looked at the maps. Time to get the lay of the land.

chapter 4

He had a whole planet to play with, but Cinch went back to the ruined village he'd inspected. There was a good reason for that. He wasn't an eidetic, but he was pretty good at remembering faces. And while the face attached to that naked woman he'd seen in the village hadn't been familiar when he'd seen it, it was after his research.

She was Chayne O'thea, once a colonel in the local army but now one of the three cutthroat leaders, could he believe the reports. She'd spent some time in the field as a soldier, commanding a platoon and then a company before being transferred to AI. Unlike a lot of people, Cinch didn't think the term "Army Intelligence" was necessarily an oxymoron—he'd met some pretty sharp folk who'd come out of one military intelligence unit or another, including a couple of rangers.

According to the recording he'd seen of the massacre at the village, the attack had been led by the red-haired pirate, Munga Vita. If that were true, why had O'thea been snooping around? Had the cutthroats joined forces? Or were things maybe not quite what they seemed?

When he was a few klicks out of the city and in a thickly wooded section of rain forest, Cinch found an old logging road and turned off the main—for want of a better

23

term—highway. The logging path was mostly plant-abate–soaked gravel and packed earth, and hadn't been used much lately. The ATV Lavan's people had supplied didn't have any trouble negotiating the track, rolling easily on four fat glassfiber tires, though the ride was bumpy. When he found a spot where some of the thick-boled trees overhung the road, he stopped the little cart.

It only took him a few seconds to discover the cart was bugged. In another minute, he had used his sniffer to pinpoint the tracking devices, there being two of them: one under the dash and spot-induced into the radioproj, the second in the frame of the cart, probably set to run off the cart's main battery. The first bug was easy, even a cursory search would have turned it up; without a sniffer as good as ranger issue, the second would have stayed a secret— you couldn't see it and it 'cast on an odd freq an ordinary scanner would miss. If somebody were looking for a tracker and they had any skill at all, they'd find the one under the dash and probably think themselves very clever; likely they'd miss the one in the frame.

Cinch grinned. It reminded him of the old joke making the rounds during the Tosh Insurrection, when the fanatical sect had been planting bombs on starships. A worried passenger asks the carrier's rep, "What are the odds of me getting onto a ship with a bomb on it?"

And the rep says, "According to the govstats, a million to one."

So the passenger says, "Well, I travel a lot, that's not very comforting."

So the rep says, "Okay, here's a way to better your odds. When you pack for your trip, put a bomb in your luggage. Chances are a *billion* to one you'll get on a starship with *two* bombs on it. . . ."

Cinch chuckled and shook his head. He'd pulled under the trees to hide from any spysats that might be footprinting him, which would seem paranoid, except for the bugs. He could knock them both out easily enough. Pull the dash bug loose and crunch it, hit the one in the frame with the fryer built into his sniffer, and he'd be clean. Then again, it was better to deal with the devil you knew than the one you didn't. If he killed both the trackers, whoever had put them into the car would know he knew he was being watched—assuming both had been planted by the same people. It was just possible that two different factions had him under loose surveillance, though he didn't think it real likely.

He reached under the dash, found the bug, and plucked it loose. It was a standard transmitter, the size of a fingernail, a bit thicker. He stepped out of the cart and stuck it to a nearby tree. It probably had a backup battery that would keep it alive for a couple of hours. He'd leave the other tracker in place. Let them think he was dull but not entirely stupid, to have found one and missed the other. It didn't matter that he was being watched.

Not yet, anyway.

Lavan was at the gym, putting in his obligatory thirty minutes on the myostim, lying nude on a padded table and watching his muscles contract in a rhythmic flow without any effort on his part. The myostim unit was set to give him a moderate workout, no point in being fanatic about these things. The peristaltic-like wave rolled up his legs and into his belly, into his chest and back, through his neck and shoulders and down his arms to his hands, knotting the muscles and then relaxing them. It didn't build any of that ugly mass the weight lifters hauled around on their frames, but it kept the body toned. Enough so he didn't have to worry about it.

"Governor?" came Pakita's voice from the doorway.

"Yes?"

"There's a com on your private channel."

Lavan nodded. "I'll take it."

The young woman brought a small com unit to the man

on the table. "Off," he said to the myostim unit. The contractions halted.

He smiled at Pakita, nude herself, as he took the com from her. He waved her away with one hand.

"Yes?"

"He found the bug under the dash in the cart," the voice said. "But the other one is still 'casting."

"Good. Where is he?"

"Headed toward Koma at the moment."

Lavan shrugged unseen at the speaker. "So? A burned-out village; there's nothing there for him to see, is there?"

"Maybe he saw something the first time and he wants to check it out again."

Lavan was unconcerned. "Don't let your paranoia run off with you."

"When the fucking Stellar Rangers are snooping around, it isn't paranoid to be worried, Yogen."

Lavan frowned at the use of his name. Vita was an idiot sometimes. Still, Yogen was a common name; there were hundreds of men who answered to it in this city alone. "It is under control," the governor said. "This guy is a plodder; the only way he is going to find anything is if he trips over it. And that won't happen if you stay out of his way."

"Maybe. But if he gets too close—"

"Maybe nothing, if he gets too close. You do *nothing*, you understand? If this doob trips and breaks his neck accidentally, the rangers will sure as hell send somebody with brains to take his place, maybe a whole shipload of them, and that is the last thing we want. If he stumbles into something he shouldn't, you call me and I will handle it."

Silence for a moment.

Lavan cracked the whip: "Is that clear? No more shooting at him."

"Yeah. I hear you."

"All right. Watch him but don't touch him. That's a discom."

Lavan buttoned the com off and waved Pakita over to take it. "On," he said to the myostim's computer. "Original setting."

Obediently, the muscles in his body began their dance again. He relaxed into the electrical massage. Vita was useful but he was too full of himself at times. He could become a liability and Lavan knew he had to watch that. He was not about to allow some hotheaded jungle trash to screw up his plans. Not a chance.

The village did not look any better on the second visit, Cinch thought. He pulled the cart to a stop, obeying the first rule of mobile transportation use and surveillance: always park in the shade. He had avoided using the air cooler in the vehicle for the largest part of the trip so the transition from the vehicle into the hot afternoon was minimally uncomfortable. It was always a good idea to acclimate yourself to the local conditions when you could—you never knew how long you were going to have to live in them. The gravity was a hair less on this world than TS, the oxy a tad more, so the overall feel was not as bad as it might have been otherwise. The usual afternoon thunderstorm was building to the southwest. Cinch saw the dark gray and purple clouds mushrooming up high enough so that the local jet stream had torn and flattened the tops. He saw flashes of lightning, but the storm pod was still far enough away he couldn't hear the thunder yet.

He walked through the ruined streets again. The breeze picked up, cooling the air as the clouds began to block the sun. He guessed he had maybe fifteen minutes before the rains arrived and this time he was prepared. He pulled his hoop-filmer from his pack and coated himself with the protectant. He had osmotic outflow for sweat and heat, but he was essentially waterproof for a while, until the film broke down. He put an extra coat on the planter's hat, to make sure he didn't miss a spot. That never seemed to fail, and in a good rain a lot of water could soak through a place as small as a demi coin.

He made no effort to hide as he walked through the village. If anything, he kept himself exposed as much as possible, using the middle of the street and pausing now and then to kick at some debris or to pick up and toss something heavy aside. He didn't yell that he was there, but if there were any eyes or ears capable of registering his presence, they would have to be dim to miss him.

As the first few drops of the thunderstorm arrived, he found an overhang in the lee of a relatively undestroyed building on the main street and sat. He leaned back against the wall and waited.

Fifteen minutes into the slashing, driving rain, the woman rounded the corner farthest from him. Unlike him, she wore no protectant he could see, though she *was* wearing clothes this time: shorts, a khaki shirt, orthoplast boots. She carried the rifle as before, but it was pointed at the ground.

"Afternoon," Cinch said, touching the brim of his hat.

She moved to stand within three meters of him, the water dripping from her soaked clothes. Which, Cinch noted, stuck to her in such a way as to be almost as revealing as her earlier nudity.

"You're Carston, the ranger," she said.

He nodded. "And you are Chayne O'thea, the renegade cutthroat." But he smiled when he said it.

She squatted, leaned the rifle against the wall so the barrel was wedged into a crack, and said, "You want to be careful of believing everything you hear," she said.

"That I do," he said. "But I want to hear as much as I need to."

"Good. Maybe when the rain stops, we can go for a nice walk."

"Okay."

The two of them sat quietly for a time after that, watching the rain fall. Cinch was comfortable with the silence, broken only by the heavy fingers of the storm drumming on the village, with the occasional boom of thunder as counterpoint. He spent a lot of time alone and it didn't bother him. He liked to watch storms, if he didn't have to be out working in them, and the overhang was fair shelter. A lot of people thought they had to fill in the quiet, but Chayne O'thea, late a colonel in the local army, did not seem to feel that need. He liked that. And without another word being spoken, he also knew he trusted her more than he did the governor. Like she said, he'd have to be careful of believing everything he heard, no matter who said it, but for the moment, the silence was speaking a whole lot and it seemed to be the truth.

He grinned. Cinch Carston, philosopher and ranger. He didn't watch himself, why, he might start writing poetry.

Even funnier, he supposed, was that once again his grandfather had been right. Before the old man died, he'd told him someday he'd find himself leaning against a wall somewhere doing more thinking than talking. And that in the doing of it, he would understand that there was wisdom in silence, too. The older he got, the more he realized that his grandfather had been a wise man. As a boy, he'd been impatient with the old man but now that he was older—not old, but older—some of his sharp edges had worn down. There was a time for sharp, but there was also a time for smoothness. Learn something new every day, the old man had said, if you pay attention and don't let it go by.

# chapter 5

The rain slacked, then stopped suddenly as if turned off at a tap. The sun resumed blasting the sodden village, and what coolness the storm had offered evaporated quickly, the heat worse now because of the air-filling humidity.

"There isn't anybody watching us in the village," O'thea said as she stood and stretched. "But my guess is that you or your cart are tagged."

Cinch wasn't ready to give too much away, but he nodded, waiting to see where she was going with it.

From a back pocket of her shorts, she pulled a compact electronic sniffer. She waved the device at him. "You seem to be clean. Must be in your cart. That would figure. The townies can't imagine anybody going anywhere on foot, so they figure you'll stick close to the cart. Come on. I've got a scooter parked in the woods a little ways from here."

Cinch said, "You aren't worried about a spysat watching us?" It was more of a joke than a serious question, but she didn't take it that way.

She glanced at a small chronograph ring on her right hand. "No, they won't have an eye over us for fifteen minutes. And it'll be an hour after that before anybody comes to check on you."

Well. The woman *had* been a colonel in AI.

He followed her out of the village and down a narrow, twisty trail into the forest. He was relatively sure somebody was watching them, her people, but he could not spot them as they worked their way along the path. His hoop film was still active, so the showers of warm drops that spattered on them every time they brushed a broad leaf or vine didn't soak into his clothes. If the fresh bath bothered her, he couldn't tell it. He guessed that natives probably got used to being wet during the rainy season, though it must give rise to a lot of fungal rashes.

Of course, the last time he'd seen her, there hadn't been any rashes noticeable on her, and he'd gotten a pretty good view.

She glanced at him in time to catch the small grin.

"Am I missing a joke?"

"Just recalling our last meeting."

"Liked my costume, did you?" She kept her face impassive, not even a hint of a smile.

"It was pretty impressive, yes."

"Camouflage," she said. "There are some groups who have gone all the way back to nature out in the bush. But the buffies are no threat to anybody, and the townies know that. If the government's sky-eye spots a naked body or two poking around a dead village, they can slot it neatly and not worry about it."

Cinch nodded, but did not speak.

After another klick or so of the serpentine slog through the wet jungle they came to a camouflage tarp draped over a small vehicle. O'thea pulled the tarp off to reveal a two-person GE scooter, what looked like a bowling pin on its side with a windshield on the narrow end, assorted controls, and a pair of saddle seats and foot pegs.

"What say we take a little ride?" she said.

"Fine."

She straddled the scooter, lit the repellors, and warmed the engines. The scooter lifted half a meter from the damp ground. "Climb on," she said.

Cinch mounted behind her, settled into the seat, and nodded.

They were another fifteen minutes in the jungle, slowly moving along a slightly wider path than the one they'd walked, then they broke into the clear over a small river. O'thea increased the scooter's speed, keeping it four meters above the sluggish brown water and following the river upstream.

Between the engines' noise and the wind, he could barely hear her when she yelled back at him. "Strap in. You don't want to fall into the bayou. Teeth eels."

Cinch didn't know what teeth eels were but they didn't sound like something he wanted to examine up close. He pulled the lap strap tight and smoothed the crow closure down.

The scooter sped over the turgid water.

"We lost him," Vita said.

Lavan shook his head. He was surrounded by idiots, people who couldn't find their asses with either hand.

The two of them were in Madam Yallaroi's Trullarium, a house of prostitution that was technically illegal but well into its fifth decade of unmolested operation. It was the largest pleasure house on the planet, the size of a small hotel, with a variety of employees catering to a wide range of appetites. Madam Yallaroi was one of three people Lavan partially trusted, and her discretion was legend. If anybody should ever ask—and anybody who knew anything about anything wouldn't even bother—the meeting between Lavan and Vita never happened.

The governor found it amusing that the old woman had given them the Jungle Suite. Faux plants and artfully placed holograms turned the room into a nearly flawless replica of the outbush, save that the floor was padded so any bouncing around on it would be as comfortable as a bed. Appropriate sound effects were included. It could even be made to rain in the room, complete with fake lightning and thunder. The wonders of technology.

"I thought you said the tracker was operative?"

"It is. The cart is parked right where he left it, but he isn't in the village. I had six of my people comb it. He's not there."

"He went for a walk in the jungle? All by himself?"

"Maybe he grew wings and flew away."

"And maybe in a year or two you can be trusted to cross the street by yourself."

Vita flushed, his coppery skin going darker. The bushy red beard didn't hide the teeth-gritting scowl.

Lavan sighed. It was like telling a small child. And he was still a little irritated at Vita for that shot at the ranger in the village earlier, even though Vita claimed he'd aimed to miss. "All right. Go and look for him. Sooner or later he'll have to return to the cart unless he plans to walk all the way back to the city. He can't do any damage wandering around out in the bush anyway. Not there."

"What about the attack on Bosset's Outpost?"

"What about it?"

"You want us to hold off?"

"Why would I want that? The ranger? Correct me if I am wrong, but Bosset's is two hundred klicks away from Koma, isn't it? You think the ranger is going to stroll over there and then stop fifty of your heavily armed people all by himself? You watch too many entcoms, Vita."

More teeth gritting. Without another word, Vita stood and stalked away, a stiff-legged march that looked comical from where Lavan sat. He shook his head and sighed. The gods should protect him from fools.

The governor reached for the drink he'd been provided. "Time?" he said loudly.

An electronic chipvox said, "Fourteen-fifty."

Lavan sipped his liquor. He had a meeting with the Finance Committee in an hour. Best he finish his drink and get back to the office. The ranger would turn up. There was nothing to worry about.

The ride on the scooter took nearly an hour. After forty minutes, O'thea veered away from the bayou and over a narrower stream that fed the river. She slowed the flight, and several times they had to duck branches that extended from the trees on the banks. In places the overhanging trees arched completely over the water to form a tunnel.

They reached a small clearing next to a lightning-blasted and downed tree that had to be five meters around. O'thea allowed the scooter to settle to the ground next to the giant root ball. The two of them alighted and she covered the vehicle with the tarp.

"We have to walk from here," she said.

"Your tour," he said.

She led him along a series of trails into a forest that grew thicker and darker. It was like being inside, he thought, the growth was so dense. Birds called to each other in the trees, mostly unseen, though he did pick out a few bright blue parrotlike ones now and then. The smell was of decay, like crushed moss and toadstools, and while the heat slackened somewhat in the deep shade, Cinch still sweated considerably. O'thea offered him a canteen she'd pulled from the scooter and Cinch was grateful for the tepid water.

After a twenty-minute walk, the trail curved sharply, running between two huge trees. When they passed through the gap, Cinch blinked in surprise.

Ahead of them was a small town of gray-green plastic domes, dozens of them, ranging in size from those large enough for only two or three people to some that could hold twenty. The undergrowth had all been cleared and the ground packed tight in the clearing. Ladders ran up the sides of the larger trees; again there seemed to be several dozen such, and at least fifty people were visible, working, cooking over electric camp stoves, climbing into the trees.

There were wickerwork buildings in the trees themselves, and bridges of what looked to be green synlin rope and stained wooden slats running between them at various heights.

All of which was fascinating, but not nearly so much so as the other inhabitants of the jungle village. Scattered here and there, on the the ground and in the trees, were several alien beings. To Cinch, they looked like a cross between gorillas and humans. They were smaller than men but bigger than chimps. They had gray, mottled skin, were relatively hairless, save for patches on their faces, heads, shoulders, and groins. The males, anyway. Some who were obviously female, judging from the breasts and lack of dangling genitals, also squatted or stood around, and there were smaller versions Cinch assumed were offspring.

He took it all in, and was aware of O'thea watching him do so.

"They are called *rangi ya majivu mtu,*" she said. "The 'gray men.' They are the true natives of this world."

"Sentient?"

"Yes. Not quite the same level as humans. Our tests show them to average around 80 on the Shisler IQ scale."

Cinch shook his head. "I didn't know anything about this," he said. "It's not in the briefing material."

"They are very shy. And they hide very well. It was thirty years after people got here before anybody could confirm a sighting. And, of course, Lavan didn't say squat about them either, did he?"

It wasn't necessary for Cinch to speak to that.

"Our best estimates say there once were almost half a million of the *majivu,* but now only a few thousand of them are left on the entire planet," O'thea said. "Most of the rest were killed by human hunters. Everybody wanted to believe they were just clever animals. That is the official policy line, you know, and most townies won't accept our test results showing the *majivu* are intelligent. And even with the most aggressive protective measures, there might not be enough of them left to maintain their species. Another couple of generations and they could be extinct."

Cinch pulled his stare away from the scene to look at her.

"Think about it. An intelligent species and hardly anybody noticed. Kind of like the dolphins on Earth, or the Sirrom on Petrie. Because they don't wear unisuits and put up buildings, they don't measure up to what humans consider 'intelligent.' Which means it's okay for men with guns to run around slaughtering them. If there is any kind of god in charge of the universe and there ever comes a day of reckoning, humans are going to have a lot to answer for."

Cinch merely nodded. That was true enough.

"This is why I quit the army, ranger. I used to be in charge of finding and eradicating the gray men. I thought they were merely dangerous animals, too, until I was shown otherwise.

"I was the leader of the genocide. Courtesy of your friend, the governor."

# chapter 6

Lavan listened with half his attention as one of the councilmen prattled on about revenue shortfalls. They were in the main conference room at the office, and the afternoon ground toward its end. There never was enough money to go around for these clowns.

It was almost dusk, and in a few minutes more, Vita and his troops were going to wipe another village off the map. A violent but necessary act, were Lavan's plans to continue their growth to full fruition. One could hardly cook gray stew without butchering a few *majivu,* could one? Pioneers had to be prepared for risks, and any that were still out there should know there were dangers by now, shouldn't they? It was their own faults if they failed to prepare themselves.

A pity, but it had to be done. Too much was at stake to turn into a bleeding heart at this stage of the game.

"—and of course, the tax code *must* be revised," the man droned one. Such a monotonic voice. Could they bottle it, they could sell it as a sleeping potion, Lavan thought. He fought to stay awake.

"You say that Lavan knows the gray men are intelligent?" Cinch said.

The woman nodded. "Oh, he knows. But acting as steward for a bunch of savages is not uppermost in the governor's thoughts."

"And what might those thoughts be more concerned with?"

She started to answer but was interrupted by a short, slim man who hurried to where she and the ranger stood.

"Chayne, Laird is on the shielded line." The slim man handed the woman a small com unit. She pointedly turned her back on Cinch as she spoke quietly into the com. Too quietly for the ranger to hear her.

Cinch and Slim looked at each other. Slim looked embarrassed.

"Shit!"

Well, that was loud enough to register. Cinch raised an eyebrow as O'thea turned around the tossed the com at Slim. "Vita's thugs are about to storm another village! Laird is on the way but he might not make it in time, he and his men and *majivu* are in crawlers." She started in the direction of the parked scooter, running.

"Where are you going?" Cinch yelled.

"I can get there by air in half an hour. Maybe I can warn the village."

"Com them," Cinch said, starting after her at a trot.

"Can't. The 'casts are being jammed."

Cinch caught up with O'thea and jogged next to her. "Won't the villagers be suspicious if their communications are jammed?"

"Maybe not. We've had a lot of sunspot activity in the last few months; it's been screwing up all kinds of electronics. They might think it's natural."

"How many attackers are there likely to be?"

"Fifty, sixty, maybe. If I can't get there in time to warn the locals, I can do some damage with this." She waved the rifle she still carried.

Cinch looked down at his gunbelt. He had three spare magazines of starfish ammo, one of armor-piercing, plus one mag in his pistol. Thirty rounds altogether, most of which wouldn't do much good against armor. He'd have to take head shots—

"What are you doing?"

He grinned at her. "I'm going with you. I'm a ranger, remember? If somebody is about to violate the villagers' civil rights, it's a galactic crime."

"You could get killed."

He shrugged. "It's my job."

After that, they saved their breath for running.

Once she had the scooter in the air, O'thea opened the throttle all the way and the little vehicle shot up and then over the jungle at a thousand meters. Cinch estimated they were doing maybe two hundred klicks an hour with the thing full out. And the village, she yelled back over the wind noise, was almost a hundred klicks away. She also spoke into the scooter's built-in com, hollering at somebody. That would likely be Laird Zarant, Cinch figured. She had to turn the com's speaker up to full volume to hear his reply and Cinch was able to catch part of it.

"—don't do it, Chayne! We're only an hour out!"

"Yeah, and according to what you said, Vita is only half that. The place'll be a smoking ruin in an hour unless somebody stops them!"

"You can't do it alone," the man's voice came back.

"I've got help. The ranger is with me."

"How do you know we can trust him?"

"He's a ranger, Laird."

"Two against fifty!"

"They don't know we're coming. We'll sneak up behind them."

"Chayne—"

"I have to go; there's a thunderstorm ahead. Flying is going to get tricky. I'll call you later."

Busy listening to the communication, Cinch had not noticed the weather, but now that she mentioned it, he saw the gray-and-purple billows of the storm directly in their path. Lightning flashed soundlessly, but he didn't know if that was because it was too far away to hear the thunder or that the airstream rushing past drowned it out.

"Stay low!" O'thea ordered. "At this speed the drops'll sting like hell."

Were it not for the string looped under his chin, he would have already lost his hat. He nodded and ducked as close to her back as he could get. She also leaned forward so the small windshield offered a bit more protection.

It stung, all right. It was like being hit with practice pellets in a combat scenario. The rain slashed at them, bouncing from his hat and bowed back. Not too bad—

A downdraft took them, and Cinch's belly went into free-fall as the scooter dropped like a stone.

"Lean left!" O'thea yelled.

Cinch obeyed, and the scooter broke free with at least ten meters between it and the tallest tree. Wind buffeted it and them, but she managed to climb back up a little higher than before.

"Nice trick," Cinch yelled.

"Wait'll you see my Immelmann," she yelled back.

He had enjoyed more pleasant rides. The wind and rain slapped at them and lightning shattered the air close enough for him to smell the ozone at one point, the thunder thumping them loudly enough so he could feel his teeth rattle.

Ten minutes later, however, they were out of the rain, and the sun shone down hard enough so the storm behind them seemed almost like a bad dream.

Five minutes out from the endangered village, O'thea dropped the little scooter to treetop level and slowed almost to a halt. She lowered the craft even more, so that it was under the tallest branches, and they crept along with foliage brushing them.

As they drew nearer the unseen village, Cinch heard the unmistakable sound of small arms fire.

"Too late," O'thea said.

"Put us down," Cinch said. "Let's see what we can do to help."

O'thea nodded, almost to herself.

On the ground, O'thea paused to check a sensor reading, then they hurried away from the scooter along an animal trail through the thick brush.

"Vita will have come from the north," she said. "That's where his hideout is. He'll have air transport in this direction."

Cinch nodded. "Well. We can't stop him from getting here—maybe we can get him to leave."

"Right."

The two of them worked their way along the trail toward the firing. The sound of an explosion louder than the shooting reached them. "They're getting cooked in there."

Cinch nodded. He'd seen the other village. But there was nothing he could do about it yet.

It took five minutes to reach the edge of the clearing where the transports were parked. Three armored hoppers the size of small buses idled in what looked like a field of potatoes or some similar crop. Each of the hoppers had a pilot inside, and there were half a dozen guards patrolling the wooded perimeter, guards wearing body armor and carrying plasma rifles. Most of the guards had their helmets off in the steamy afternoon, and even so, they must have been baking in the hardshell armor. The hoppers were mostly buttoned up, except for one: the pilot had opened the kleersteel plate window next to him so there was a handspan of open space next to his head. And the fool had also removed his helmet. He was smoking a flickstick.

The driver was about 150 meters from where Cinch and O'thea lay crouched in the bush, give or take five meters, the ranger guessed. He pointed at the hopper.

"Can you make that shot from here?"

"I can make it."

"Okay. Give me two minutes, then cook him," he said. "I've got to get closer to do anything with this." He waved his handgun.

"Two minutes."

Cinch scrabbled off into the bush, keeping the clearing to his left as he circled closer.

It was fairly quiet here, but the shooting didn't seem that far off, maybe a klick. There was another explosion as somebody spent more ordnance at the village. *Come on, Cinch, get it in drive—*

He was hidden pretty well and maybe thirty meters from the nearer guard, two of them standing in profile to him, their weapons pointing at the ground. Long way for a head shot, but it was as close as he was going to get. He stretched out prone, lit the red dot sight, and brought the tiny glowing circle up until it was centered on the closest guard's temple. He took a couple of deep breaths and slowed his heart as best he could. Should be about ... now ...

The flat crack of a plasma rifle echoed across the clearing and before either of the guards could react, Cinch pressed the trigger on the Smith. There came the sharp *whoosh* of the propellant gas, then the sound of the missile breaking the sound barrier, a flat *crack!*

A hundred and forty-eight grains of metal hit the guard's temple, pierced the bone, and mushroomed into a malignant starfish, plowing a tunnel through brain tissue. He'd be effectively dead before he reached the ground.

The second guard twisted toward the sound of Cinch's shot but he didn't drop, he crouched, and Cinch had already lowered his weapon in anticipation. As the plasma rifle came up, Cinch found his target and fired again. He had aimed at the center of the man's forehead but he was off a little. The bullet smacked into the guard's left eye.

Cinch rolled, gun still extended, covering ground like a human wheel.

A toothy hail of bullets chomped at the ground where he had just been, chewing up plants and spewing dirt.

Cinch rolled to the base of a meter-thick tree, the only cover dense enough to stop a plasma round. But they were still shooting at where he had been before.

He leaned out far enough to see that three of the pedestrian guards were down, the two he'd shot and another one. Of the pilot in the hopper with the open window, there was no sign.

Two of the remaining troopers on foot had managed to get their helmets on and visors down. As he watched, a round from O'thea's weapon spanged off one of the helmets, knocking the man down but not penetrating the spidersilk hardshell. Cinch's own AP for his pistol would work on softsuits, but not on military-grade hardshell. But for the confusion it offered, he put the last four rounds of the starfish in his magazine into the other trooper's helmet. It was enough to make the man scream and dive prone, at least long enough to worry that he might be in trouble.

The other trooper still up was running toward the nearest hopper screaming for the pilot to open the door. He had dropped his weapon and his helmet dangled unremembered in his hand as he ran.

Cinch did a quick magazine change, but the running man was probably ninety meters away, too far for a pistol shot unless he was real lucky—

The running man's head exploded, red spraying as if a firecracker had gone off inside an ink-filled balloon. O'thea. She was good to hit a moving target that small from where she was.

Cinch scooted back from the edge of the clearing. One of the hoppers opened up with a motorized gatling, and the jungle at eye level was suddenly filled with buzzing metal that chopped down everything in its way.

*Time to leave the party, Cinch.*

He half crawled, half ran in a low crouch toward where he'd left O'thea. Behind him, a tree half as big around as

Cinch toppled under the slashing AP claws of the hopper's gun. A few hundred 20mm expended uranium slugs flying at two thousand meters a second would do that.

He saw O'thea heading his way, also moving low.

"I think that's all the damage we can do here," Cinch said.

"Yeah. The pilots'll have commed the storm troopers. They'll be coming back to protect their ride."

"We might pick a few more off," Cinch suggested.

She shook her head. "Negative. We're way outgunned. Laird'll be here soon. Let's get out of sight."

Cinch nodded. There was a good idea. He moved, but through some trick of the brain, he remembered, too. The first time he'd ever shot anybody.

He'd been young, not yet twenty-two TS, before he'd seen the error of his ways and joined the rangers. He'd been smuggling a load of contraband liquor, working with two other young men who thought they had the galaxy by the balls, who were stupidly fearless, who were going to live forever. They had outfoxed or outrun every cool in the sector, were laughing about how easy it was to make the police look stupid when the pirates hit them.

Pirates were worse than cools. Pirates stole from people who weren't going to go running to the authorities for help because what they were doing was illegal. Uh, well, you see, they took this shipment of peach liquor we were smuggling . . .

Yeah, right.

The pirates waited until they docked the borrowed lighter, waited until the customs idiots were satisfied, then rolled in with their hardware out. He would have kept his hands in the air and let them take it. It was only money, it was part of the game; sometimes you had to deal with shit, and tomorrow was another day. But Denjie lost it. He pulled his weapon and the pirates opened up on him. There had been four of them against their three. It never did get totally clear for him. One second he had his hands in the air smiling and being philosophical about losing their cargo; the next second he was pulling his pistol.

Denjie went down, chest torn open by a pirate's sleet-gun.

Mandel got off a magazine or most of one before the pirates killed him, and with it, he took out three of the four.

The last pirate iced Mandel, turned toward him, and Cinch filled with coldness as if liquid nitrogen had been pressure pumped into him. Tachypsychia, he learned later, but in that moment, he knew he was going to die unless he stopped it. The pirate was fast but he had to refocus himself on Cinch after he did Mandel. Cinch had only the one target to consider, and he was faster.

He didn't remember the sounds of the shots or that he'd emptied his weapon into the pirate and still kept pulling the trigger. They were close, five, six meters apart, and all of his shots punched into the pirate. His back, when he fell onto his face, was one huge crater.

Cinch stood there for an eon. Maybe longer.

One of the pirates moaned, wounded but still alive.

Cinch's mouth went dry, his heart hammered, trying to get out of his chest, and he ran to Denjie, then Mandel. They were dead. So were the other pirates, except the one who moaned, and he looked to be going fast.

Cinch ran. To hell with the shipment . . .

Here, next to O'thea, he was a well-seasoned professional and that first time was long years past. He had faced worse, had shot to protect himself, had assassinated men from ambush as he had just done. And not once had it ever been any easier. Shooting men wasn't something you got used to, not if you had any kind of conscience. Sometimes you had to do it, there wasn't any other solution. But even when it was the last resort, it was always hard. Even now, his mouth was dry and his heart was still rumbling along too fast. Being right didn't make it any easier. Dead was forever.

# chapter 7

The governor sat and listened to the council's prattle for as long as he could before excusing himself. Lavan was soaking his tired buttocks in the heated gel of the rumble spa when the call came in from Vita. He'd been expecting the man's com and he leaned back into the undulating gel as he established the connection.

"Good evening," Lavan began. "Things went well, I trust?"

"Not so good and not so well."

Lavan sat up straighter. "What do you mean?"

"I mean somebody was laying for us. As soon as I got my people into the, uh, target, they hit our transports. Took out a bunch of my troops, almost got the hoppers."

"What?!"

"A big force, fifty, sixty of 'em. Well armed."

"That's impossible! There aren't any military in the area."

"Who said they were military?"

Lavan ground his teeth. "All right. Who were they?"

"Don't know. We fought our way out, collected our own dead and wounded, but we didn't have time to stop and chat, if you know what I'm saying. But they had to know about the attack beforehand; they hit our transports before we got warmed up in the village."

"Damn."

"Yeah, you got that right."

Lavan considered the import of what Vita was saying. Who could it be? Zarant? O'thea? It had to be them—they were the only other groups out there with enough on the beam to shoot it out with a force the size of Vita's. And they would do it just to aggravate him. But how had they found out? More importantly, what was he going to do about it?

"Patch up your forces and wait until I call you," Lavan said.

He clicked the com off and looked around. He had forgotten he was in the tub during the conversation. He stepped out of the swirling tub and sluiced the gel off with a towel. Damn. First the ranger, now this. From years of political infighting, he knew there were always things that could crop up and block his path, but he usually anticipated them and moved accordingly. This was unexpected. He expected spies in his organization, but who were they? Probably in Vita's camp.

Well. He had some spies of his own he could activate. He hated to use them, because they wouldn't stay secret for long and they were expensive and time-consuming to replace, but that's what they were there for, weren't they?

Damn.

By the time Zarant and his troops arrived, the battle was over.

Cinch and O'thea moved into the village after Vita's thugs hustled back to their transports and lifted. It was bad, but not as bad as the other village Cinch had seen. The diversion he and O'thea had created had been enough for the attackers to cut short their stay. Fourteen local people had been killed, two dozen more wounded, some serious, some minor. Somebody had gotten lucky with a hunting rifle and taken down a couple of the attackers. The town's doctors had survived the assault and were busy caring for the injured. Cinch and O'thea offered first aid and helped put out fires. All in all, the village had been fortunate, considering the alternative.

Zarant's transports arrived and his people began pitching in.

It was well after dark before the last of the fires was extinguished and the wounded attended to. The call for outside help had yet to produce results.

Cinch was spraying water on a section of burning wall when O'thea arrived with company. The power had been restored and outdoor lighting lit, so he had a good view of the man behind her as they walked to where Cinch stood.

Big, he was, and built like a weight lifter. He wore raggy khaki shorts and sandals and a large sheath knife strapped around his waist, nothing else. The muscles in his chest and shoulders were thick and heavy, and his hair was black and cut in a squarish mane that hung almost to his shoulders. Like Vita, another bodybuilder type.

"Cinch? This is Laird Zarant."

Cinch wiped sooty sweat from his forehead, then cleaned his hand off on his own shorts. He nodded at the big man.

Zarant's deep and calm voice was a match for his body when he spoke. "Ranger. Chayne says you did good out here today." He waved at the wounded village in a broad gesture with one hand.

"If we had gotten here ten minutes earlier, we might have kept them pinned in their transports," O'thea said.

Zarant shrugged. "You work with what you're given." To Cinch, he said, "We appreciate what you did. I'd hoped to meet you sooner under a little more pleasant circumstances." He grinned at that.

Cinch thought about it for a couple of seconds. He returned the grin and said, "The hypo gun. That was yours, wasn't it?"

Zarant's smile grew. "How'd you figure that?"

"Somebody wanted to talk to me. If they'd wanted me dead, the gun wouldn't have been loaded with sleep chem. All the local authorities had to do was ask and I'd go see them. O'thea and I bumped into each other before, if she'd wanted to say something then, she had the chance. Vita is a killer and we wouldn't have anything nice to say to each other. That leaves you." It wasn't flawless logic, but it was fairly clear. And it was coupled with a hunch.

Zarant nodded. But there was something else behind his eyes, and Cinch decided to check and see if he could find it.

"But my guess is, if the trap you set had gotten me, you wouldn't have wanted to talk to me either, is that right?"

Now Zarant laughed and extended his hand. Cinch took it and they clasped each other's forearms. Nothing wrong with the big man's grip.

O'thea said, "Am I missing something here?"

Cinch said, "Zarant had somebody set up a deadfall in my room. Hypo gun aimed at my front door. If I had opened the door wrong, I would have taken a forced nap and waked up with a headache. What I realized was, it wasn't so much a trap as a test. If I were unwary enough to get shot, I wouldn't be much use."

"No offense intended, ranger, but you are smarter than you look," Zarant said.

"No offense taken, and so are you. And you can call me 'Cinch.' "

"Maybe we could find a quiet spot and talk," Zarant said.

Cinch nodded. "Okay."

He was here to get the lay of the land, and so far, he'd met all the major players but one. When he saw that one, he wanted to do it in his gunsight, whatever else was going on. And he was pretty sure by now that whatever *was* going on, it was not exactly the same as he'd been led to believe.

Well. Welcome to the rangers, pal. Sometimes people lie to you.

Big surprise.

"I can't do it!" The voice was barely a whisper on Lavan's com, even with the sound turned all the way up.

"You damned well better do it."

"If I get caught—"

"—they'll probably execute you," Lavan said. "You never thought of that before?"

"I . . . I, well, yes—"

"If you don't do it, I'll see to it that they find out about you anyway. Then they will *know* you're a spy. Do it my way, look sharp and watch yourself, and nothing happens—except that you get to keep collecting the fat stipend I pay you."

There was a long silence.

"Well?"

"Couldn't I just leave a com transmitting and you home in on it?"

"No. Their signal is umbrellaed and bounced off a satellite rigged with a diffuser. We can't trace it to a location any nearer than fifty klicks."

Another silence. Then, "All right. I'll do it."

"Good. Discom."

He was about to cut the link when the spy said, "What about the ranger?"

Lavan blinked. "What *about* the ranger?"

"He was here. At the compound. He went with Chayne to the village."

Well, well, that was news. But he said, "I know that. Don't worry about the ranger, we'll handle him. You just find out what I want to know."

Lavan frowned at the comset as he killed link. Bad news, all of it. First, it *had* been O'thea and that hulk Zarant who had bollixed Vita's operation. No real surprise there, but according to his spy, Zarant's troops couldn't have gotten to the village in time to stop Vita. Had O'thea and the ranger potted a few of Vita's men and panicked him? Was that story about being outnumbered and having to shoot his way free nothing but pigshit? He wouldn't put it past Vita. The man was brave when the odds were on his side, but looking too far down the road at his personal gain to risk his neck without being certain he wouldn't lose it. Vita wanted to look good more than anything.

So. The ranger had found the opposition and connected with them. That was bad. He was smarter than he appeared, and it also appeared that Lavan might have underestimated the man. That was bad, too. Mistakes like that could get you in deep trouble in a hurry.

Well. No matter. He had held off longer than he should, not wanting to create martyrs who might be used to stir the sheep. His spy would find and transmit the exact coordinates he needed and Lavan would have the army fall on the rebels like a mountain of lead. They would be crushed and end of problem. No more troublemaking monkey huggers, no more gray men, no more obstacles. And there wouldn't be any public record of the raid; it would buried in a "Planetary Security" file, so no martyrs.

Now he smiled. All that had gone before was merely a glitch, a small error that, in the end, would mean nothing. Hardly worth remembering.

# chapter 8

Cinch went with Zarant and O'thea in Zarant's crawler, along with five other humans and two of the gray men. In the confined space Cinch noted that the apelike creatures had a pleasant, somewhat spicy odor he hadn't been aware of before. O'thea's scooter was strapped to the back of the segmented crawler, which chugged along on electrically driven treads much like a mechanical version of a centipede. The vehicle's windows were open to the air, but a blower cooled the interior enough so it was bearable inside. Even under the shade of the tree canopy, it was still warm out there.

One of the gray men leaned close to Zarant and spoke. The creature's voice was soft, the language a liquid flow broken occasionally by glottal stops and sibilants that shaded into whistles.

Zarant nodded and spoke to the gray man in the same tongue. Cinch heard his own name mentioned.

The gray man nodded and turned toward the ranger. He said something else and extended his hand.

Cinch kept his face impassive, nodded, and put his own hand out. He clasped forearms with the gray man. The gray man smiled and Cinch mirrored the expression. He'd waited for that. In some cultures, a showing of teeth was not meant to be pleasant.

"K(!)ree," the gray man said. He half swallowed, half clucked the first sound into a click.

Cinch glanced at Zarant but the big man kept his face deadpan. Another test? Probably.

To the gray man, Cinch said, "Nice to meet you, K(!)ree." He gave what he thought was a passable imitation of the word. He hoped his guess was right, that it was the gray man's name. "I'm Cinch Carston, of the Stellar Rangers. Might translate to C(!)arston—" Cinch tried the click on his own name.

The gray man laughed, turned toward Zarant, who also smiled.

"C(!)arston!" Kree said, obviously pleased.

"So it would seem," Zarant said.

Kree turned back to Cinch. "Pleezed to meetcha, C(!)arston!"

Cinch blinked. Kree spoke passable Galax; he'd heard people do worse.

Well, well. Learn new things all the time.

A flyover of the village showed the fires to be out and the locals nursing their wounded buildings. Of the attackers who had thwarted Vita's attack there was no sign.

Lavan brooded as he watched the holoproj. His spy had still not sent the coordinates to the hidden encampment and the governor was a bit irritated. It was always something going wrong. Why couldn't things go like he wished? *Damn.*

It was well after dark when the crawler arrived in the vicinity of the jungle hideaway. Cinch was travel-weary and ready to stretch his legs. Which was good, since they still had another ten-minute walk to reach the clearing. He was glad somebody else was leading, because the jungle was like the inside of a deep cave. He had his spookeyes in his belt pouch but since nobody else seemed to need augmentation, he left them there.

Zarant was just in front of him and Cinch said, "Why park so far away?"

"No high-tech engines allowed in the compound," he said. "The *majivu* don't much like 'em and we don't want to abuse their hospitality."

"I thought maybe it was because a good simadam might pick up a repellor's signature in a low flyover if the sensing gear is tuned right."

There was enough light for Cinch to pick up the flash of teeth as Zarant grinned. "That too," he said. "Better they should drop their bombs ten minutes away from us."

Cinch walked in silence the rest of the way, considering the situation. He couldn't be sure of things yet. True, O'thea had been willing to risk her neck to save a village from a slew of murderous attackers. And Zarant seemed genuinely concerned about the fate of the indigenous population. Even so, that didn't mean the governor of the state was behind either the attack or the extermination of the gray men. Cinch's natural inclination was to distrust politicians generally, and to believe somebody he'd just risked his life with, somebody who had covered his back when the guns spoke. A woman who was willing to run around naked to fool a spysat was surely smart, but that didn't necessarily make her honest, even if he might want to believe it. According to a study he'd once read, a trained observer with years of practice could tell the truth from a falsehood when it was offered by a really good liar about fifty percent of the time. About the same as flipping a coin. He grinned to himself in the deep night. His gut instincts told him that Zarant and O'thea were trustworthy, but he was a ranger and he had to have more than that. He would keep poking around until he knew more before he made a final decision. Getting all the facts about the depth of the water below before you leaped into it from a great height was always a good idea.

* * *

The morning sun found Lavan at Service with the other worshipers. He was hardly a believer in any kind of deity, benevolent or otherwise, but a lot of people were and they voted. He could look as pious as the next man when it suited him.

The faither spoke in parables. He spoke of mercy, justice, he spoke of balance. All things that most people did not get in life and things that Lavan suspected they didn't get in death, either. Well. Balance, he supposed. All the dead were the same, weren't they? Someday he was going to be among the dead and it was his intent to delay that day for as long as possible; more, since a lifespan of 130 or 140 years was really quite short when compared to how long he was going to be dead, that is to say, forever, he intended to enjoy his life to the fullest. They were doing some experimental work with cloned bodies and memory transfer on Wu and did a man have sufficient money, he could assure a place in the line to get the technology when it was perfected. That might take another twenty or thirty years, from what he had heard. And it would certainly take a major fortune, not just a piddling few million cees like he had. With the money he had now, he could live another sixty or eighty years in relative luxury. To extend that when the breakthrough came, he needed to be in the billionaire class, and even so, there were already dozens of the super-rich ahead of him. But he would get there in plenty of time.

Assuming that Vita, Zarant, O'thea, and the ranger didn't screw things up, of course. His cart might be a bit wobbly, he thought, but it was still basically on-track. The call from his spy could come at any moment and he had the com in his pocket set to vibrate rather than make any sound when it did come. It wouldn't do to disturb the faither's litany with the harsh chirp of an incoming call to mass murder, now would it? When he felt the buzz of the com, he could excuse himself from this boring lecture on

love and harmony and the Cosmic Parent and get the legitimate military operation to wipe out the cutthroat bandits
into the air. Unlike Vita and his irregulars, the army would
do the job right. They could operate out in the open, with
the full weight of the law behind them, and while it might
make nasty headlines, in the end it would be done and
there wouldn't be anybody who could do anything about
it. With the rebels and ape lovers gone, the plan to take all
those protected lands and sell the mineral and other natural
resource rights to an offworld corporation would proceed
quickly. With his credit tab fattened considerably in the
bargain, under the table, of course. Two, maybe three
months, and he'd have his bundle and be off to a better
world and to hell with this planet.

If the ranger had to die in the doing of it, well, too bad.
He could conjure up a pretty scenario for the man's
bosses. Heroic figure, helping the troops subdue the rebels,
a tragic loss during the battle; he'd even give him some
kind of posthumous award or somesuch. That ought to
work. There would be plenty of witnesses to the ranger's
unfortunate demise. Yes. That could work nicely; he certainly had the skill to manage that bit of business.

Lavan shifted on the uncomfortable bench. He suspected
the seat had been made deliberately hard and ill-suited for
sitting to keep the churchgoers awake, given the lack of
fire in the speeches usually given in the place. The faither
droned on, painting a picture about the goodness of man
and the pride of the Cosmic Parent in its children. Lavan
grinned. Right. He had no patience with fairy tales, but he
was a good politician. He nodded now and then and was
aware of his fellow citizens' noticing how attentive he
seemed to be. Might as well keep up the charade until the
end. You never knew what might happen. Best to keep all
one's options open.

Cinch's bed, an airpad in one of the tree houses, had
been quite comfortable. He awoke at first light, relieved

himself in the small chemical-unit fresher, flushed the tiny room with ozone, and washed his face and hands. He'd stayed in worse places, more than a few times.

By the time he walked out of the tree house to the small deck, the compound was beginning to stir. Here and there a few of the gray men were up and about, as were a human or two . . .

Off to one side of his tree, in a cleared area of the compound, he saw Zarant, still dressed only in shorts, moving in a rhythmic and slow martial dance. Cinch watched the big man as he dipped and bent, kicked and thrust, turned, all as if he were mired in thick air. *Diegee,* the dance seemed to be, or one of the variants. Cinch himself was a practitioner of *denku-te,* the hard and fast fighting art of "lightning hands." He was hardly as expert as his own teacher, the legendary Master Sissu, who was reputed to have once fought the equally legendary *sumito* dancer Saval Antoon Bork to a draw in a friendly match, but he knew a few moves. Enough to realize that Zarant was very good at what he was doing down there. It was harder to move very slowly with precision than it was to move fast, a thing that most good fighters knew and that most would-be fighters did not understand. A man as big as Zarant who could move that well was very impressive. Perhaps more impressive was the fact that the big man had half a score students trying to ape—most of them literally in this case—his motions. All but one of the students were gray men. The remaining dancer was O'thea, and her grace seemed nearly a match for Zarant's.

Cinch watched the form, and raised one eyebrow as he realized the most impressive thing of all was that Zarant had tailored the form so that it suited the bodies of the *majivu* more than it did the two humans performing. Many fighting styles copy animals in their dances. The crane, the bear, the snake, the tiger were more often seen in *dojos* or *kwoons* these days than they were seen in zoos, metaphorically speaking, at least. But this form was decidedly an

ape *kata* or *kuen,* and it looked more natural on the *majivu*
than it did on the humans. *Very* interesting.

Cinch didn't know how long they had been exercising,
but the dance continued for another fifteen minutes as he
watched. When they were done, all the students bowed to
Zarant, who returned the bow. Then they broke and moved
off, with O'thea staying to talk to Zarant. After a moment,
the two looked up and saw Cinch watching.

"Nice work," he said.

Zarant nodded. "Come on down, I'll buy you breakfast."

Cinch returned the nod. He was hungry; he couldn't remember the last time he had eaten. Breakfast sounded
great, even if it was roots and twigs.

It turned out to be the local equivalent of ham and eggs,
with hot bread, fruit juice, and real coffee. Cinch was
pleased with that.

The three of them sat near one of the small stoves
where a cook was turning out more of the same for other
early risers. The morning was warm but not yet uncom-
fortably so. "Only time of day you can really eat a hot
meal in the summer," Zarant said, after he finished a
mouthful of food. "Nobody feels much like cooking when
the air temp is hotter than body heat."

"I can understand that. What was the style you were
practicing?"

*"Chi-tai shu'wan.* My uncle was a teacher. Before humans arrived on this world, the *majivu* had no word for
'war.' And outside of a mild chest-beating ritual the males
did at mating season, more show than action, they didn't
fight each other, either."

"And you're teaching them how to do both."

Zarant flushed under his dark tan and nodded, his face
grim. "Yes." He paused a second, then continued. "They
aren't like children, the *majivu.* They have a history, a rich
culture. It's not like human culture, but it's there. They are
intelligent enough to understand what has happened to

them since men arrived here, intelligent enough to see their own end unless something is done to stop it. But even so, what I find myself doing doesn't bring me any particular joy. I'm responsible for giving these people something they never had before. Never needed before, true, but I don't want to be a guru, any kind of authority figure, at least not on this level. Sure, I taught students, human students, but none of them ever looked on me as any kind of savior."

Cinch nodded. A big responsibility. He didn't think he'd have the shoulders to support that weight.

Zarant wiped sweat away from his forehead with the back of one hand. "They aren't children. They are more innocent than children. And I'm the man who has to corrupt that innocence, to paint for them and make them see the ugly picture of reality. They have to have it to survive, but I wish there were another artist. It isn't a fun job."

Cinch didn't speak to that. What could he say?

# chapter 9

They were just finishing breakfast when trouble arrived, running. A short woman with gray flecks in her long black hair sprinted into the dining area.

"Laird, we've got a radio transmission from inside the camp!"

Zarant jumped up. "Shit! Where?"

"Looks like the south quarter, we can't pin it down any closer than that."

"Go! Chayne, evac-one!" Even as Zarant spoke he was running.

"Right!" O'thea split off and headed to the left.

Cinch stayed with Zarant.

"You think there's a spy in camp?"

"Got to be. No UA radio transmissions are allowed; nobody in that quarter is supposed to *have* anything that will transmit."

"Where are we going?"

"South quadrant. It's probably too late but maybe not."

The two men ran. Behind them, a siren began wailing, a demented electronic warning scream impossible to ignore if you had working ears.

Just ahead, a group of small prefabs, one slightly farther away than the others. Zarant ran toward them. People and

60

gray men came out of some of the structures, running, dragging on clothes, carrying children. If Cinch hadn't figured it out before, the runners would probably have given it to him. They knew what the alarm meant and they weren't wasting any time stopping to ask each other what the hell was going on.

"That one!" Cinch yelled, pointing at the farthest building.

"How do you know?"

"Nobody is coming out of it."

Well. It was as good a reason as any to head that way. Surely a spy wouldn't be doing his business in the middle of a bunch of people?

The two of them ran. Zarant was ahead and he hardly slowed as he hit the door with his outstretched hands, palms flat.

The door was thin plastic, designed to keep out weather and flies, maybe small animals, but not a charging hundred-kilo-plus man. The door vanished as it slammed open on its hinges.

Cinch was a half second behind, no more, but by the time he arrived, he saw Zarant smash into a table and do a fairly nice somersault over it to slam against the far wall of the building.

The man he'd seen when he first arrived, Slim, was it? was scrambling to the side. In one hand he held a small com unit; Cinch was able to see a green diode showing that the unit was powered up. In the other hand, he held a small pistol, slugthrower or a dart gun, maybe, and he was bringing it to bear on Zarant, who bounced from the wall, shook the whole structure, and came to his feet, trying to turn toward Slim.

Zarant was unarmed and too far away for his martial arts training to be very useful.

Cinch snatched his pistol from its holster, yelling to distract Slim even as he made the draw. "Drop it! Rangers!"

The yell was enough to catch Slim's attention. He

started, twisted, and tried to swing his weapon away from Zarant to point at Cinch.

"Drop it, drop it!" Cinch finished the draw. Slim was no more than five meters away. He shoved his pistol at Slim in a punching motion. "Drop it!"

Slim got off a round. From the twang, which faded even as he heard it, Cinch realized it was a spring gun. Probably electric or poisoned needles. Then the tachypsychia effect took over. Cinch's vision tunneled, left him a circle that included the gun, Slim's upper body and face, no more. Mostly the gun. Sounds vanished. Time dilated, expanded, slowed, so that a quarter second seemed to be all day. Years. Eons.

Cinch fired, twice. The threat was the gun and while it wasn't his intent, the first starfish bullet smashed the gun, tore it from the hand holding it, knocked it back against Slim. The second round of the double tap zipped past the empty hand and found Slim's chest, right over the heart.

Slim fell in slow motion, arms going wide, the com unit flying up and back. The clatter as it hit the wall was the first sound Cinch heard since the spring gun fired, all those years ago, back when the universe was young.

Time sped up, seemed to run too fast for a second, then settled down to normal.

"Fuck," Zarant said. He jumped for the com, picked it up and thumbed the power switch off. He looked at the dying man on the floor.

"Stupid." He shook his head. Then he looked at Cinch. "We better move. I expect we have company on the way."

Cinch nodded, and the two of them hurried out of the prefab.

Lavan's computer locked the coordinates into memory and told him it had done so.

The governor smiled. Now he had them. "Call Colonel Neeture," he ordered the computer.

"Neeture here."

"I'm sending you the coordinates for the cutthroats' hideout, Colonel. I would appreciate it if you would pay them a visit at your earliest convenience." He tapped a control and the modem launched the numbers.

"Got it," the man said, the words snapping out crisply. "My drop teams will be in the air in forty-five seconds. It'll take us . . . half an hour to get there, tops."

"Glad to hear it. We aren't interested in paying for costly trials and imprisonment, Colonel. Not for animals like these. You understand."

"Copy, Governor. I'll call you when we're done."

Lavan smiled at the computer. Well. That was that, wasn't it? An hour from now, two, and most of his problems would be over. The weather forecast was calling for heavy showers most of the afternoon, but, Lavan decided, it was going to be a great day despite that. A great day.

The evacuation was orderly once it got moving seriously. Cinch watched as the youngest and oldest members of the camp were loaded into aircraft, onto scooters, whatever would move them away in a hurry. The rest of the group piled into the land vehicles. Cinch joined Zarant in the last of the crawlers to be loaded. O'thea was leading the children and ancients' air caravan, so Zarant said.

The vehicle lurched into motion and began to follow the other returning crawlers. About as fast as a man doing a warm-up jog.

"How long before the military gets here?" Cinch asked.

"Forty minutes from the nearest tactical base, if they dawdle. Thirty if they hurry. I expect they'll hurry."

"How far away can we get in that time?"

Zarant grinned. "Not far enough. Once they realize there's nobody home under their guns, they'll spiral out and search. The kids and grannies will be okay, well out of range by then. In the bush crawling on trails, we can't get more than eight, maybe nine klicks away."

Cinch absorbed this. Zarant didn't seem particularly

worried about being flattened under a military assault. Cinch said as much.

Zarant grinned wider. "I like you, ranger, you pay attention. They will be able to do a flyover easy enough, but they probably won't spot us, for the same reason they haven't spotted us before. We've got state-of-the-art confounders on the crawlers. Under the canopy, our camogear will keep us invisible. With the confounders running, we don't put out anything they can lock onto. No heat signature, no radar or doppler sig, zip. As long as we don't shoot or yell too loud at 'em, they won't know we're here."

"Unless they put men on the ground and do it the old-fashioned way," Cinch said.

"Yeah, there's that. But this is our jungle. And you know how cheap the military is when it comes to outfitting line troopers. We'll be able to see them coming, they won't be sporting confounders, just standard camouflage. My simadams can spot a pulse rifle at half a klick. Our side will have the advantage. *If* they put troops on the ground."

"You think they won't?"

He shrugged. "Maybe. They usually don't. Squads and whole platoons have been known to . . . disappear into the jungle and not return. They like five-to-one odds and a straight-up fight," he said. "They might have the numbers but they can't see us and that makes 'em nervous. I think they'll stay in the air."

"That's a fairly risky supposition."

He shrugged again. "Yeah, well, that's what we have to work with."

Almost an hour went by before the copilot working the crawler's scopes said, "Here they come."

Cinch heard the sound of jet rotors overhead as copters went past to his right. It was hard to judge distance under the thick canopy but he guessed the aircraft were at least five hundred meters away.

"Not even close," the copilot said. "And looky here, we got us a rain pod moving in. Another ten minutes and we catch a nice electrical storm to give the few and the proud something to think about."

The copters crisscrossed them several more times, once passing almost directly overhead, near enough for Cinch to see the eye-confusing lightboard camouflage that was the ship's belly.

"Your electronics are pretty good," Cinch said.

"Yeah, they ought to be. They cost us a fortune, money we can't afford. At the moment, I'm inclined to be glad we spent it, though."

It took a while for the rain to filter through the thick green canopy but the sound of thunder and the occasional flash of lightning told them the storm was there.

In another ten minutes, the sounds of copters buzzing by like giant mechanical mosquitoes faded.

"My guess is that we're home free," Zarant said. "Me, I wouldn't want to be the officer in charge of this little foray, not when he tells Lavan we got away." He laughed.

"Where to now?" Cinch asked.

"Fallback base, about eighty klicks southwest of here. We set up, start over again. The gray men have lived there off and on for centuries and nobody ever found 'em."

"Search everybody for radios?"

"Yeah. That too."

Cinch nodded. He hadn't figured on getting into the middle of a war when he spaced to this world, but he had learned that trying to figure too much in advance sometimes got you into trouble. Better to deal with the reality than your expectations.

That had been a major flaw in the way he thought for years. Old Debbil Expectation always lurked out in the darkness, just beyond the range of the fire. About the time he thought he had gotten past expecting things to be a certain way and then being disappointed when they weren't, the demon would find itself a new disguise and come sneaking back into camp.

Don't I know you? Cinch would ask.

No, no, we've never met.

And because the face was altered, the voice deeper or higher, Cinch was all too ready to convince himself that this wasn't an old demon but maybe a new friend. And every time, *every* time, it came as a shock when the mask was dropped and the nasty laughter started.

Fooled you again, didn't I, Cinch? When are you ever gonna learn? A man has to take things as they come, not as he *wishes* they would come. C'mon, Carston, how hard can this lesson be? How many times do I have to slap your face before you get it?

Cinch grinned at himself. That question came back to haunt him a hundred times, maybe a thousand times. He wasn't sure he'd gotten it yet, but he was getting better at unmasking his demons.

At least he liked to hope so.

# chapter 10

If Cinch thought the jungle he'd seen before was heavy, the new terrain made it look like somebody's clipped lawn. There were places where the trees were so dense they seemed to be a solid wall next to the carved-out trail. The canopy was a jumble of leaves, vines, fungi, laced by the sounds of birds and other animals who preferred the trees to the ground. They had long since switched on the vehicle's lights, for it was like driving inside a hot, damp, fecund cave.

"There are places here where a good climber can travel twenty or thirty klicks without having to set foot on the ground," Zarant said.

Cinch nodded. "I believe it."

They had shut the coolers off to save fuel and the windows allowed the hot and moist air into the vehicle through thin mesh screens. Insects thumped against the barriers, trying to get inside.

"You'll want to use a chemical shield or repellor when you go out," Zarant said. "Flies and mosquitoes will suck you dry otherwise. We had a bugfield generator at the old campsite but not where we're going."

The crawler groaned along in relative silence for a time, the gloom outside hanging like thick moss under the trees.

67

"Real heart of darkness stuff, isn't it?" Zarant said.

Cinch was somewhat surprised at the literary reference. He shifted and looked directly at the bigger man. "What brings you into this?"

Zarant sighed. "Well. You might not think it to look at me but I used to be an anthropology professor. Ensconced nice and safe in my academic enclave, writing monographs on noble savages. I grew up here and I knew about the *majivu* of course, but like almost everybody else, I bought the official line about them being animals. Then one day I was talking to a group of river rats on the Lower Mzaha and one of them told me the creatures were brighter than most people he knew. That wasn't saying much, given the company he kept, but I heard the same thing from others. So I decided to check it out."

"And you found they were intelligent."

"Eventually, when I finally did find them. It took the better part of a year of trying. And I also found them to be gentle and even spiritual, in their own way. Until man arrived here, they lived in harmony with this world, a natural part of the ecosystem. They are so shy that even some people who have lived in the outback for all their lives have never seen a gray man except from a distance. They can't protect themselves against men with guns and evil intent. There is no word for 'murder' in the *majivu* language, did you know that?"

"So you took up their cause."

"Yes. I was like a lot of pseudo-liberals in the colleges where I worked; I prided myself on being a champion of the underdog, like that. But I never really did anything about it." He chuckled. "I guess I was like a reformed click addict once I got going. You know, nothing worse than somebody who has rid himself of a nasty habit and wants everybody else to do the same. I got pretty self-righteous. Obnoxious, too. When I realized nobody in power wanted to hear what I had to say, that my coms and letters to the editor and PAC rallies to Save the Gray Men weren't doing the job, I decided to try a . . . more direct approach."

"So now you're an outlaw. Long way from a college professor."

Zarant shrugged. "Sometimes you have to take a stand. It's the right thing, no matter what the law says otherwise. History is full of people who chose to be moral rather than legal."

Cinch nodded in return. Law was important, of course. It tried to lay some kind of reasonable order on chaos, but sometimes things slipped through the cracks. Justice and the law were related; at times they were twin brothers; but other times they were distant cousins—you could hardly see one in the other. As a ranger, Cinch knew what Zarant said was true enough. If everybody obeyed all the laws, even the bad ones, humans would still be on Earth, probably working for the great-great-times-fifty grandfather of the first king who'd stood up and claimed to be in charge.

No, ethics got situational, there was no way around that. Cold-blooded murder was almost always wrong, but now and then, it wasn't. There were monsters who masqueraded as people and a clean death was too good for them. Cinch had met a few such folk. Shot a few of them, too. When you were out on the frontier, you had call to be more than a peace officer in certain situations. Judge, jury, executioner, those weren't his favorite roles, but he could play them if need be.

Whether that was needed here he still wasn't sure, but this planet had good people who would strive to do the right thing if they could. He'd have to see how it all worked out.

Lavan was not pleased. Had he a gun in his hand, he would have shot the damned colonel without a second's hesitation.

"You lost them. After I personally gave you their exact location."

"Sorry, sir, but there wasn't anybody there when we arrived. We found your coordinates fine, but the camp was almost empty."

"And you didn't bother to look for them? How far could they have gotten in the thirty or forty minutes it took you to arrive? I know they were there when I called you."

"We looked. They must have had air transport. Our sensors came up clean."

"Sensors? You didn't put men down into the jungle?"

"No, sir. We arrived shortly before an electrical storm. It was raining buckets and there was no point—"

"No point? Excuse me, did I hear you say there was 'no point'?"

"Governor, they were gone. It is a big jungle, thousands of kilometers worth. I had two companies, a few hundred men, there was no way to search it all, even if they could have seen anything under the deluge. That storm dropped eight centimeters of water in just over an hour."

"Colonel, I don't care if it dropped a meter of battery acid! You let them get away."

"With all due respect, sir, I got my people to the site exactly when I said I would and the quarry had already bolted. We found one man in one of the huts and he was shot dead."

"One man. ID on him?"

"Sir." The Colonel handed the governor an infoball. The seated man shoved it into his computer's reader. The air lit with the image and stats.

*Well, fuck.* It was his spy. Ex-spy. Somebody must have overheard him 'casting the location and taken him out. *Damn.* Wasted him for nothing.

"That's all, Colonel. Leave."

After the colonel was gone, Lavan pondered his options. He'd have to get Vita back on it. They were going to have to use stealth to catch the cutthroats and their ape friends and that wasn't going to be easy. Vita, for all his faults, was a fair tracker. If the recently departed rebels had left a trail, maybe Vita could find it. This was beginning to be more than a little irritating; it was rapidly becoming a major thorn in his foot. *Dammit!*

He reached for the com.

When the crawler arrived at the new camp, the brush thinned into a clearing in which the trees were less densely spaced on the ground. Cinch couldn't tell about the canopy; it was well past dark and hard to tell how much light would filter through during the brightest part of the day. The driver powered down the crawler and it got very black.

Zarant handed Cinch a sprayer of insect repellent and used a similar one on himself. Others in the vehicle also applied the chemicals to themselves and the sound of the sprayers and a smell of gingerspice filled the crawler.

Seated in the back the gray man K(!)ree made a barking sound suspiciously like a laugh. When Cinch finished his chore and looked at the gray man, K(!)ree was holding his nose and grinning.

"All smell like dead *samaki* all over in here!"

Zarant said, "Bugs don't seem to bother the *majivu* much."

"Pee-yew!" K(!)ree observed. He waved one hand as if to clear away the odor.

Zarant pointed his finger at K(!)ree. "Hey, when you can dress in a sheath and cravat and sit through three hours of boring speeches at a formal faculty dinner, *then* I'll be impressed, foghead."

K(!)ree only barked louder.

"You'll note the *majivu* have a sense of humor," Zarant said, his voice dry. "If canted somewhat toward the slapstick end of the spectrum."

Outside the crawler Zarant produced a pair of flashlights, handed Cinch one. Other small battery torches lit, the focused beams stabbing into the thick gloom.

"This way," Zarant said.

Cinch followed him. The darkness pressed in on them. Without the lights they carried, it would have been almost total.

The ranger was aware of some members of their party splitting off—the sound of their muffled footsteps on the thick humus grew quieter—until only he and Zarant and K(!)ree continued to slog over the soft ground. After a few minutes they reached the base of one of the baobablike trees. Against the side of the big trunk was a synlin rope and plastic slat ladder. Cinch climbed behind Zarant for what seemed a fair height before they reached a branch as wide as a sidewalk. The top of the branch had been shaved or planked so that it was relatively flat and Cinch trailed along behind Zarant—K(!)ree had disappeared ahead of them—until they reached a platform upon which was a good-sized hut, the roof freshly thatched with still-green leaves and vines.

Zarant waved the flashlight. "Your suite," he said. "Since we're a little pressed for space, you are sharing this *nyumba*. Get some rest and we'll talk in the morning."

"Thanks."

Zarant turned and moved back down the branch toward the tree's trunk.

Cinch played the flashlight's beam over the tree house. As nearly as he could tell the oval-shaped hut—what had Zarant called it? A *nyumba?*—had screened windows and a door, probably to slow the onslaught of bugs. A good idea. Despite the repellent he wore, a number of insects had bounced off him on the short walk and climb, and others buzzed close enough that he could hear the high-pitched hums as they tested the chemical he had sprayed on himself and his clothing.

He reached for the screen door and opened it, moved inside quickly to avoid leading a swarm of insects into the place. He noticed two things once the door shut behind him: there was a dim lightbar mounted along the wall three meters up that cast a pale and indirect light about that of a good-size full moon, and—

Chayne O'thea, bathed under a makeshift shower near the far curve of the oval wall, gloriously wet and naked. The trickle of water ran down her tanned body as she looked at him, flashed him a quick grin, not looking the least embarrassed at her nudity. "Evening, ranger. I'll be done in a second and you can have the shower."

Cinch thought about turning away and decided that if it didn't bother her, he'd just as soon look. And she was something to look at. The perfect curves of her buttocks, the flow of her legs, the high and firm breasts. Even her face looked good, wet hair and all. Good bone structure. He could look at her for a long time and not get bored.

But showering in front of O'thea might not be a real good idea. That was the difference between men and women: he couldn't tell how she felt by looking at her naked but she certainly would be able to see what was on his mind if he shucked his clothes. He hoped the water in the shower was cold. Real cold. Otherwise, if he wanted to keep his thoughts to himself, he was going to shower facing the wall.

And not too damned close to the wall, either . . .

chapter 11

If O'thea had any interest in watching Cinch shower, he couldn't tell it. She dried off with a cloth towel—no blowers here in the jungle, it seemed—slipped into a thin silk shift that more or less covered her from shoulders to knees, and moved to one of the two pallets laid out as beds. She stretched out on top of the sheet on her back and closed her eyes.

Cinch considered his modesty. He'd been seen naked by more than a few women in his life, and it had never bothered him. Of course, those were usually medics or women he had just made—or was about to make—love to, so this wasn't quite the same.

Still, he was dirty, sweaty and covered with bug spray and the idea of a shower was compelling. He stripped, piled his clothes by the second pallet, and padded across the woven-mat floor to the jury-rigged shower stall. This proved to be a single pipe entering through the roof, ending in a shower head, along with a simple mechanical on-off valve just above the head. The mats had been cleared from the floor, and there was a circle of thin plastic sheeting with a drain in the middle.

Cinch opened the valve and a weak spray of tepid, not cold, water flowed. Hardly a needle blast but sufficient to wet him and wash away the thin lather from the bottle of liquid soap he found on the shower's floor. It took almost five minutes to rinse away the grime and spray and he felt a whole lot better when it was done. His beard would need depil in another day or two, but his face was smooth enough until then. He picked up a folded towel and dried himself, and the rough absorbent cloth felt pretty good against his skin. Given that O'thea had apparently drifted off to sleep and was now less than fully naked, Cinch's worry about his own state of visible arousal had, well, flagged somewhat.

He wrapped the towel around his hips, finger-combed his hair, and padded across the mat to the second pallet. Even after the shower the night was warm on his skin and he pulled the towel off and lay down on the pad. He used the sheet to cover himself to the waist. He had a lot on his mind but he was also bone-tired. It had been a long, strange day. Sleep stole over him but before he drifted off, he heard O'thea say, "Night, ranger."

Well, shit. She'd been awake all this time.

Did that mean something? If it did, did he want to know?

He felt the presence of Old Debbil Expectation, heard the laugh outside the range of the campfire's light.

No, you don't. Not this time. I see you there, comrade.

You're mistaken, the voice called back.

I don't think so. Fuck off.

Hollow laughter surrounded him.

He dropped off to the buzzing of an insect who'd managed to sneak inside the hut.

Vita was not far from outliving his usefulness, Lavan thought. The big redhead sat in a chair across from the governor, more of a sprawl, actually, grinning at him.

"So your hotrocket soldiers fucked it up, hey? They couldn't find their butts with both hands and radar. Hell,

they were lucky—Zarant and his apes would probably
have kicked their asses anyway."

"Thank you for your helpful opinion," Lavan said. "You
feel better now?"

"Yeah, I do. Given that you're asking me to go find the
monkeys when your plasma pluggers couldn't do it, I feel
pretty good."

Definitely getting close to the time when Vita would
have to retire from life. Lavan put a sting into his voice:
"I'm not *asking* you, Vita, I am *telling* you. Don't forget
who runs this operation."

"It's my neck on the line!"

"So it is, and you are well paid to risk it. And if we pull
this off, you'll be able to spend your days counting your
money and patting yourself on the back. But as long as
Zarant and O'thea and the gray men are out there running
around, our offworld friends will be too nervous to put
down their roots. And until that happens, the prize is out
of reach. Am I making myself clear here? Is there some
part of what needs to be done you don't understand?"

Vita flushed, angry, but he held it in check. "No. I know
what needs to be done."

It was late and Lavan was tired. He waved one hand at
his hired thug. "Good. Go and do it. Call me when you get
some results."

Vita left, tried to swagger, and only managed to look
silly. Lavan shook his head. Vita was getting ambitious,
starting to act as though he were a partner instead of an
employee and that couldn't be allowed. Once he tracked
down the cutthroats, Vita's usefulness would definitely be
over. There was a new public building going up in a few
weeks. Lavan wondered how Vita would like spending the
next hundred years or so as part of the plastcrete founda-
tions of that structure. With any luck at all, Lavan would
be around when the as yet unbuilt edifice was razed, the
workers found the body and wondered over it. A pleasant
fantasy, that.

* * *

Cinch awoke as O'thea, once again naked, began to dress. He blinked sleep away and watched as she efficiently slid into her shorts and shirt. She was aware of him watching, for she said, " 'Morning."

He supposed that in time he could get used to seeing this woman without her clothes to where he wasn't aroused by it. Yeah. Maybe in a couple of thousand years.

" 'Morning," he said. "What time is it?"

"About 0600. You have an appointment somewhere?"

"No."

She finished dressing, nodded at him. "See you later."

After she left, Cinch pulled the sheet off and stood. He walked to the chemical toilet, used it, then got dressed himself. Much longer out here and he'd have to figure a way to clean his clothes; they weren't the freshest things he'd worn.

Outside on the limb the morning's light turned pale as it filtered through the thick canopy, a dim gray-white hardly enough to cast shadows. Two hundred meters away, Cinch saw what looked like the bank of a fair-sized river. Amazing. Last night he hadn't gotten a hint of that.

There were others up and about, people, *majivu,* going about their business, whatever it was, and nobody seemed to be paying any attention to him. Cinch meandered down the thick limb to the nearest rope ladder and descended to the ground. Once there the river was out of sight, but he worked his way in that direction.

It took about ten minutes to reach the bank of the river. The water flowed past at a good clip, five, maybe six klicks an hour, and was a turgid muddy brown. Where he stood, the river was about a half klick wide, which probably qualified it as a major waterway in these parts. To his left, well back from the bank and hidden from the air under the trees, were several small boats. Looked like electric siphon motors on a couple of them. Beyond that was a small bay where the river cut into the bank, a semicircular pool with a sandy beach lining it under the shaded overhang of some palmlike trees. A woman stood on the sand watching four children, two human and two *majivu,* splash in the gently swirling pool. The children looked to be about six or seven TS years old and they had a big air-filled ball they tossed back and forth.

Cinch smiled. His grandfather had taught him how to swim when he'd been a boy, probably about the same age as those four. The old man had been a water-sailor at one time in his spotted past and was as good a swimmer as Cinch had ever seen.

"Lotta sailors, they don't swim," his grandfather told him as they sat on the edge of the pool. "They figure, ship goes down a thousand klicks away from land, what's the point? Me, I always figured that the point was to stay alive a little longer and see what happened. It's always a good idea to have options, you understand that, Rudy? A choice. You don't like swimming around in the ocean waiting, you can always let go and drown, but at least you have a choice."

The boy Rudy had nodded. He was still twenty years away from his ranger nickname. "I understand, Gramps."

"Good. Let's go try that sidestroke again."

Cinch smiled through the memory at the children laughing in the water. Been a long time since he'd thought of learning how to swim.

He started to turn away from the river and head back toward the interior of the camp. A woman's screams stopped him.

One of the *majivu* children was out of the eddy and into the river. Cinch quickly saw why. The ball had been thrown past him—or her—and the child had swum after it. The current had them both now, and while the child obviously could swim, he or she wasn't making much progress against the swift flow.

The woman was already in the water, legs churning in a knee-deep run as she headed toward the child.

Cinch's mind snapped the image and made automatic calculations. Too slow, the kid would be a hundred meters ahead of her by the time she reached the main flow. And the child would sweep past where Cinch stood in a matter of seconds, too far out for him to reach or extend a branch. Nothing to throw to the kid—the boats were too far away.

Cinch pulled his shoes and socks off, unhooked his gunbelt—no time for the pants and shirt. He took a few steps and launched himself into the water in a racing dive, praying there weren't any just-below-the-surface snags or rocks.

The water was warm, the current strong. He came up, blinked, and saw the *majivu* child coming toward him. Cinch was a powerful swimmer but the current was too powerful to resist fully. What he did manage to do was swim against it enough so that he moved downstream much more slowly than the struggling child. It only took maybe thirty seconds for the child to come within reach.

"Easy!" Cinch yelled. "I got you."

He looped one arm around the child, who clamped both arms around his. Good. He treaded water and allowed the river to push them along for a moment, then started a long and angular swim toward the shore.

The trick to swimming in an undertow or strong river current was not to struggle against it. Cinch's grandfather had taught him that. You might not be able to swim against or even across a riptide or a river, but you could use it and gradually angle your way out of it if you didn't panic. Cinch did the lifesaver's sidestroke, holding the *majivu* child—a little girl he could tell now, since she was stretched out on her back on the surface—with one arm, using a scissors kick and shallow arm pull with his free hand.

It took four hundred meters before he was back to shore again, another fifty meters until he found a shallow spot where he could wade ashore.

He set the little girl down, squatted next to her, and grinned. "You okay?"

She nodded, her eyes wide in fright.

"Well, that was fun, wasn't it?"

She shook her head from side to side.

"No? Oh, well, never mind. You don't have to do it again if you don't want to."

That brought a timid smile from her.

By this time, other people and gray men began arriving at a run. One of the *majivu* males snatched up the little girl and hugged her, clicking at her in their own language.

The first human to arrive was O'thea. She let out a sigh and shook her head. "Damn."

"She's okay," Cinch said. "Little scared, that's all. She did a good job, didn't panic; she just wasn't strong enough to buck the current."

"Lucky you were there."

He shrugged.

"You did good, ranger." There was a second's hesitation, then, "Cinch. You did better than you know."

Cinch looked at her.

"The *majivu* value their children above all else," she said. "You just became a local hero. They'll be singing songs about you around the campfires from now on."

The male who had clutched the little girl put her down and came over to stand in front of Cinch. He reached out with both hands and took Cinch's right hand in his, bent his head to touch it to their hands, then looked up and rattled off a phrase full of glottal stops and clicks.

Cinch nodded gravely, not understanding.

"He says he owes you his future," O'thea said. "He doesn't speak our language."

"What's his name?"

"K(!)lua."

"Tell him I know he would have done the same for my child if I had one. One takes care of the children, all of the children."

O'thea nodded and clacked at K(!)lua.

The *majivu* smiled broadly. He squeezed Cinch's hand hard enough so the ranger worried about his bones, then released his grip and threw his arm around Cinch. "C(!)arston!" he yelled.

The other *majivu* echoed his name.

"You just made a whole village full of friends for life," O'thea said. She smiled at him. "And you can include me in that."

Cinch returned the smile. It was early but the day seemed to be off to a pretty good start. He'd also figured out a way to clean his clothes, though maybe next time he would take them off first.

chapter 12

When he saw Zarant a few minutes later, Cinch was still in the center of a dozen of the *majivu*. The smaller gray men made the ranger feel like a vid star, and a giant one, at that.

Zarant had a mixed group of people and *majivu* around him and he grinned at Cinch. "You've made an impression on the People, ranger. There's not a one of them who wouldn't climb through a spike bush for you right now."

Cinch shrugged. You didn't let children drown where he came from. "What are you doing?"

"Bringing another shipload of forbidden fruit to the Garden."

Cinch didn't speak to that but raised an eyebrow in question.

Zarant said something in rapid *majivu* and the gray men scattered, running to bushes and trees. Thirty seconds passed and they were back; now they carried long rods, some of them; others had several shorter sections of the skinny sticks—about as big around as his little finger— which they assembled by snapping or screwing them together. The finished batons were nearly as tall as the *majivu* were.

From the biblical reference Cinch figured the staves had

**82**

to be some kind of weapon but they didn't look particularly imposing.

"They going to beat the mosquitoes to death with those?"

Zarant's face grew grim. "Not exactly. K(!)ree."

The gray man loped to where the two humans stood and handed Cinch the rod. Plastic, had to be, it was so light. Then Cinch saw that the lightness was because the rod was hollow. Like a weapon barrel. And that one end had an hourglasslike swelling on it. The material was too thin to allow an explosive charge of any real power to be used, but Cinch realized what the propellant would be, given the level of technology the *majivu* had to work with.

Air.

He handed the tube back to K(!)ree and nodded at him. To Zarant he said, "Blowguns."

"There is a lizard that lives in the bush called *upesi kifo;* it's a bright yellow and you can see it twenty meters away. Little thing, eight or ten centimeters long, no teeth or claws. But nothing in the jungle bothers *upesi kifo* because when it gets excited it secretes a pale liquid from under its skin. It's a paralytic nerve toxin. Get it in your mouth or a cut and you have about twenty seconds before your lungs seize up. There's no antidote. I've taught the *majivu* how to use blowguns whose darts are tipped in the lizard venom. They can all hit a man-sized target anywhere inside fifty meters. In the jungle, that's plenty of range."

Cinch nodded. "You have to use what's available." He paused, then, "So they've got weapons. Will they use them?"

Zarant sighed. "Yes. If they are attacked, they will defend themselves. Now I know how the serpent must have felt if he had any conscience."

Cinch thought about it for a second. "If the alternative is their own deaths, I don't see how there is a whole lot of choice. The longer men are on this world, the more likely they are to extend their civilization. The *majivu* will run out of places to hide eventually."

"I know. But the death of any intelligent being isn't something to feel good about."

Cinch shrugged. In his experience, there were some who were better off dead—humanity was safer that way—but he understood the theory. Despite his looks and what he was doing here, Zarant was basically a pacifist. It must be miserable to have to subvert those principles by active military resistance. Bad enough he had men in the jungle with guns; now he was having to equip the natives, who had never needed weapons before humans arrived on their world.

Print out another hard copy for the sins of man file.

And what was he, a Stellar Ranger, going to do about all this?

Lavan was, he had to admit to himself, worried.

Perhaps it was merely a coincidence that the ranger's arrival had somehow stirred the insurgents into a greater activity. But since the ranger had plopped himself down on the planet, things had not gotten any better. He had a backup plan, of course—the one thing politics had taught him was that you *always* had a backup plan—but he hated to use it. It was risky and if it went wrong, the ranger would certainly become his enemy, if he wasn't already; still, the situation surely called for stringent measures.

Lavan leaned back in his plush chair and sighed. Yes. Do it.

Time to call the Actor.

One of the big advantages to being governor of a world was the number of resources available to you if you needed something official. Lavan left his ceremonial body-guard posted outside his sometimes-used hotel suite while he slipped out the back way. He had used quikspray to darken his hair and beard to black, and a few dabs of quikstik to stretch and hold his facial features into those of somebody else, certainly not the governor, thank you. Along with a cheap set of coveralls, ugly boots, and a little artfully applied bearing lube, he could pass for a flitter mechanic or maybe a port loader. He made his way to the scanshop where he would meet the Actor.

The sun beat down on the city, adding a humid hammer to the heat. God, he hated this world. He was never going to spend any more time on a tropical planet once he got away from this place. Temperate, all the way, that was the idea. Oh, maybe a winter sojourn to one of the ice crystal palaces for variety, but no more sweaty worlds.

Under the weight of his disguise and the warm afternoon, Lavan walked, not too fast, not too slow, just at the pace a tired mechanic going back to his cube after a tough shift would set.

The scanshop did cheap printout work, mostly, some layout and mixed media. It wasn't wildly successful, but the extra income the owner got from Lavan helped, and running a small business was preferable to being in prison, which was where the owner had been until Lavan commuted her sentence for counterfeiting. And where she would be again if she didn't do exactly as he demanded.

He grinned. Power was interesting, and no fun at all if you didn't wield it once in a while. What was the point in being a giant if you didn't squash a few little people every so often?

There were two customers in the shop, haggling over the price of wedding invitations. An employee tended to them while a second flunky ran a high-speed laser printer in one corner. The owner, a squarish woman of forty, sat at a desk, working on a flatscreen.

She looked up and saw Lavan. She knew who he was, of course, and a scowl danced across her face before she could hide it with a fake smile.

Lavan's smile was real enough.

She stood and waved him into the privacy of her office.

Inside, he sat in the chair behind the desk and leaned back.

"You have my documents?"

"I have them."

"Let me see."

She moved to the desk, pointedly waited until he slid back to afford her access to the center drawer, then removed a cloned sharkskin wallet from the drawer. She handed the wallet to Lavan.

He opened it.

The Actor's face stared up at him from behind a clear plastic window.

Lavan removed the ID and inspected it. According to the visual on the shimmery-rainbow plastic card, the Actor was one Sedih Peran, Inspector-at-Large for the Stellar Rangers. There were official-looking seals and signatures and magnetic code strips and it looked genuine enough.

"How good is this?" He waved the ID card.

"It'll fool any reader we have on this planet. The security info code matches that on the ID you gave me to use. It will fluoresce to match the original, it's got the anticopy strips embedded, and it should pass a chemical analysis anywhere except a galactic-class lab. Unless whoever you plan to fool has got better resources in his back pocket than we have on this whole world, he won't be able to tell it's a fake."

Lavan smiled. "I knew I could count on you."

"Yeah, well, I've got work to do, if you don't mind."

"Go ahead. Somebody is meeting me here in a few minutes."

That earned him another scowl, at which he smiled all the wider.

The shop owner left and Lavan went through the rest of the items in the wallet. A couple of hundred cees, well-worn local currency, ones, tens, and twenties. A folded commendation from the head of the Stellar Rangers ten years ago, for "services above the call of duty." There was a hardcopy printout of a validated starliner ticket, listing arrival and departure times. The final item was a holograph of a cold-looking woman and two not particularly handsome preteen children, a boy and a girl. On the back of the picture it said, "Sedih—All our love—Dinjin, Ikan & Muka." The picture showed signs of much wallet wear.

A nice touch, the picture. Not that the ranger was apt ever to see anything but the ID; still, it paid to have some depth in these things. The Actor was good enough that he might contrive a way to leave the wallet where the ranger could examine it.

Lavan shoved the ID into the sharkskin wallet and tapped it against his knee. The beauty of the scheme was that the ranger couldn't check it out. Oh, well, he *could,* but radio lag being what it was out here in the backrocket lanes—they were light-weeks away from the nearest ranger station—it would take some time before he could get it done and discover the IAL was a fake. Using any resources he could command on Mtizito, the ID would seem valid. Even if he did get a message to the nearest ranger station via the hottest Salinas courier he could find, the ranger would have ceased to be a problem long before an answer arrived.

The Actor would play his part well enough, Lavan was sure of that. The Actor was a devotee of the hypnogagic method. Within a certain framework and with some portion of his brain, he would believe he *was* a ranger inspector come to pull Carston's fangs. Strongly enough, so he had told Lavan, to pass a simple lie detector or even a light electropophy scan. If the ranger happened to have stress analyzer in his kit, the Actor would sail right past it. So he said.

Lavan tended to believe him. The man had never failed him before.

Speak of the devil.

"Ah, good afternoon," the Actor said. He flashed perfect teeth in a truly warm and gracious smile. "So good to see you again."

Lavan, despite his knowledge, believed the smile and words. Amazing. The man could sell bloody beef to vegetarians.

"And you," Lavan said. "Let's have a little talk, shall we?"

The Actor smiled. Of course.

Cinch had basically seen what he'd come to see. He'd met with the planetary authorities and two of the three supposed-rebel leaders. The one called Vita wasn't likely to be available, according to what Zarant and O'thea said, and he tended to believe them. If they were correct, then Vita was in league with Lavan, the governor, and dealing with him might prove dangerous.

As he watched the gray men and humans going about their business in the new campsite, he considered his next move. Maybe it was time to go back to the city and do some more digging. There was always a trail, could you but look closely enough to see the signs, and surely the bad guys on this world would have left traces he could find. As far as the governor was concerned, he was a ranger doing fieldwork—Cinch was pretty sure he could convince the man of that—and no problem to them. *If* they were guilty of anything. That remained to be proved, although he personally believed much of Zarant and O'thea's story. Belief was not courtproof evidence.

Cinch nodded. He was done here. Time to move on.

"Cinch?"

He turned and saw O'thea standing there. "Yes?"

"I was wondering if I might speak to you alone?"

"Sure."

"I've set up a tree house, over that way."

"Okay."

He followed her toward the new structure, a foamed building already stained to match the surrounding vegetation. A rope ladder led up to the small irregular-shaped cube. Cinch followed O'thea up the rope, once again marveling at the view of her backside as he climbed. They reached the hut and she opened the door, let him pass next to her, then closed the door and shoved the latch into place, locking it. It wasn't much door, but the lock would hold against a casual pull.

"What can I do for you?"

In answer, she stepped close to him, raised herself up on her toes, and kissed him passionately, her tongue seeking his own.

Cinch's eyes went wide, but only for a second before he closed them and returned the kiss in earnest. With utmost enthusiasm.

Somehow they managed to remove their clothes without falling down. Then they did fall down, after a fashion.

She was strong, muscular, wet, and very hot. He tried to touch all of her at once, hands sliding over her shoulders, back, buttocks, kissing her furiously. O'thea did the same for him.

By the time they reached the floor, they were both ready and he filled her with himself and lost all conscious thought in the dance of dances.

# chapter 13

Cinch grinned as the naked O'thea leaned over and bit his shoulder lightly. "Ready again?"

He laughed. "Not quite. The four-times-in-an-hour Carston is history. I can remember him dimly—from about twenty-five years or so ago."

"Well. Three isn't so bad, especially for an old ranger."

"Thank you. Not that I'm complaining, mind you, but—what brought this on?"

"You're not gonna tell me you weren't interested?"

"Nope, not me, ma'am. I was interested from the first moment I saw you and we sort of almost met, Fem O'thea."

"Yeah, I thought so. And you can call me 'Chayne' now, M. Peace Officer, sir. To tell the truth, I wasn't interested in you that way. You sort of grew on me. First when you pitched in against Vita's bandits. Then when you jumped into the river and saved the child, that brought it to a head. So to speak."

"You mean it wasn't my stunning good looks?"

She slid one hand down his chest, lower, used her fingernails on him lightly. "Not quite dead, I see."

"Just gathering its strength."

"Hmm. I wasn't aware you had any looks to speak of until I watched you shower at the old camp."

"You watched?"

"Sure, just like you did me."

He grinned again.

"I mean, you're kind of . . . average looking, you know? Put you in a room with two other people and you disappear."

He nodded. "Professional trick. Comes in handy when I do sub rosa work. Old ninja technique."

Now she laughed. "Right."

"No, I'm serious. I can blend in or stand out as needed. Next time you see me in a crowd, watch. I'll show you."

"You're on. Although I don't expect I'll be seeing you in a crowd anytime soon. Given our current situation, being close to more than a handful of people mixed with *majivu* might not be very healthy for somebody of my status."

"Things change."

"So they do. My, my. Look at this. What can it be, handsome?"

Her fingers continued their flickery dance on him.

"I thought you said I was plain."

"Handsome is as handsome does," she said. "I wanted you for what you are, not what you look like." She bent, lowered her head, and found something most interesting to do with her mouth.

Cinch's brain went away again.

"How many messages does he have?" Lavan asked.

Pakita made a sound with her mouth like a wine bottle being uncorked. She blinked and looked up from her current task. "You want to know that *now?*"

"When you're finished. And you almost are."

It only took her another few seconds to prove him right.

Amazing woman, Lavan thought. How did he ever get along without her?

She stood, wiped her mouth with the back of her hand, and padded naked into the outer office. The door of which was quite securely locked, of course.

"The ranger has four messages," she said when she returned. She slipped her glowsilks on, adjusted them. "Three from you, one from somebody named Sedih Peran, who calls himself an I-A-L, whatever that is."

Lavan shrugged, as if he hadn't a clue.

Pakita left the inner office and went to unlock the outer door. Lavan watched her sensual, hip-rolling walk, liquid and loose. A thing of beauty, no question.

Sooner or later the ranger would check his com for messages. When he did he would discover that someone in authority over him had come to visit and if he had any sense whatsoever, he would hie himself back here to see who the man was and why.

Lavan scratched idly at a spot on his left arm. Had something bitten him? No, no bite marks he could see, just an itch.

He'd done enough research through his contacts offworld to determine that while most rangers of any longstanding service were apt to know each other, if not by sight, then at least by reputation, IAL officers were beasts of a different color. They were charged with keeping the Stellar Rangers honest, the galactic equivalent of local police forces' Internal Affairs, and as such, kept to themselves. They were not looked upon favorably by other rangers, the IAL, and they kept a low profile to avoid exposing themselves to "accidents." They were, of course, a necessary evil, as were all such watchdogs. Someone had to police the police. The rangers were supposedly more honest than most agencies. The IGDEA—Iggy—the Galactic Marshals—Goonies—and the Delivery Service Ops—Dipsos—were all notorious for taking bribes to wink at drug deals, prisoner escapes, and pilfered packages. While the rangers didn't have that kind of reputation, there were always a few bad peaches in every basket.

Probably Carston had come into contact with IAL before, but he wouldn't know all of them, and thus the Actor could manage him. Once he found out what the real ranger knew or suspected, they could deal with it then. Maybe the guy really was a fumblefoot and he had fallen into the cutthroats by accident. The Actor could send him on his way, direct him into a dead end and everybody would be happy. Well. At least Lavan would be happy and that was what counted.

If, on the other hand, Carston proved more clever than expected, or if he were obstreperous, then he would be dealt with as necessary. It would be no trick at all to prove to anybody who came looking that the ranger had left the planet in a privately hired ship that, alas, developed engine difficulties and fell into the sun.

He truly did not think that Carston was bright enough to see through the Actor, now that he had considered it at greater length. The Actor had once fooled his own mother into thinking he was a stranger, and a woman, at that.

No. The offworld interests would find fertile ground when he reeled them in and took their money, and nobody of consequence would be in the way.

Somebody had rigged a communal shower and after Cinch used it and shaved, he felt more than a little relaxed. He asked to borrow one of the cycles.

Chayne said, "Sure. How come?"

"I've got to get back to civilization and do some more snooping."

"You believe us about Lavan and Vita?"

"Yeah, I do. But if I'm going to call in a galactic prosecutor, I need more than that."

Zarant wandered over, still in nothing but shorts and bug repellent.

"Cinch is going back to town to dig up some dirt on Lavan. Evidence."

The two of them exchanged looks gravid with something Cinch couldn't quite identify.

After a moment, Zarant said, "We might be able to help you some there. Chayne says we can trust you."

Cinch looked at the woman, who flushed red under his gaze.

"And you trust her," Cinch said.

"I hope so." He gave Cinch a big grin. "She *is* my wife, after all."

Cinch sucked in a quick breath, but before he could say anything, Zarant went on. "Open marriage, Ranger. I trust her judgment in that department, too."

Cinch nodded, once. Okay. He'd been involved with stranger things; still, it was a surprise.

"We have a contact in the city, somebody who might be able to supply you with what you need to staple Lavan's skin to a wall."

"I'm listening."

"If our operative can get what you need, how soon do you think you could move against Lavan? Time is a critical factor."

"It'll take a few weeks to get a galactic prosecution team here, along with enough marshals to back them up, in case Lavan decided to fight it. We don't arrest planetary governors that often. He could call out his own troops. We could have a war on our hands."

"But he would have others things on his hands than the *majivu* and their lands if the galactics came to town, wouldn't he?" That from Chayne.

"I'd expect so."

"A few weeks is a whole lot better than years of running and hiding in the jungle," Zarant said. "Okay. I'll give you a number. Com it when you get to the city. You're pretty much our only hope, ranger. If you can't stop Lavan, sooner or later he'll hunt us all down and wipe us out."

Cinch nodded. Not much he could say about that.

\* \* \*

When he was a hundred klicks away from the camp and spiraled away from it enough so nobody could backwalk his route, he called the comcomp. He had five messages, three from the governor's office, one from an IAL, and one from somebody who wanted to service his flitter at bargain rates.

IAL. Damn.

Like most rangers in the field, Cinch had been tabbed by IAL now and then. You had to be a little more careful with rule bending when one of the hamsters was looking over your shoulder. They got the nickname from a small rodent, the females of which, when disturbed, sometimes ate their newly birthed young. You had to be careful with rule bending anyhow, but out on the frontier, sometimes a literal interpretation of the law might be less than just. Or wise. Not with the hamsters around, though. You toed the line or you got a nasty report for your file. If you had a decent commander, the report got duly logged and then stuck in a Möbius routine and never accessed again. Decent commanders came from the field and they had dealt with the hamsters themselves. The last time Cinch had gotten a black screen from IAL, his chief, Sector Commander Ingmar "Hacksaw" Harvey, had called him into his office.

"Got a report from IAL on you," Hacksaw said. "Courtesy of the IGDEA."

"Yeah?"

"Seems you physically assaulted an Iggy agent on Roget."

Cinch nodded. "Yep. A flat punch to the solar plexus and then a hammerfist to the back of the head. Put him facedown in the dirt and out cold."

Hacksaw looked at the flatscreen, shook his head, said, "Did he deserve it?"

"In my opinion."

Hacksaw tapped the screen and blanked it. "IGA thinks

I should reprimand you harshly for damaging relations with our brother agency."

Cinch shrugged.

"You ought not to go around beating up on Iggy ops, Cinch. I mean, working for IGDEA is punishment enough for anybody." Hacksaw grinned. "You suppose that's a harsh enough reprimand?"

Cinch raised an eyebrow.

"Come on. I'll let you buy me a beer and we'll consider that your fine."

"You're a hard man, Hacksaw."

"Yeah, all the women tell me that."

Cinch grinned at the memory. But Hacksaw was getting close to retirement and who knew but that the next SC would be a stuffed shirt. Better see what the hamster wanted.

After another few minutes of aimless circling, Cinch pointed the scooter to where he'd left his cart and headed back toward civilization.

Although after listening to Zarant and watching the *majivu,* he wondered just how civilized they really were back there.

# chapter 14

Cinch put in a com to the IAL. He wasn't available, but
the comcomp told him the man was staying at the best hotel in the city.

He must have money of his own—the rangers didn't
mind if you traveled first-class, as long as you paid the
difference; they sure didn't offer a per diem thick enough
to cover luxury expenses. Unless the hamsters had something going he hadn't heard about.

Great. Just what he needed. An inspector with a rich
man's sensibilities. Inherited, too, most likely, since you
didn't amass wealth as a ranger at any level, and a self-
made rich man wasn't apt to leave a successful career to
become a peace officer.

Cinch grinned as he piloted the ATV toward his own
room. He wanted to shower with hot water and get into
some really clean clothes before he went to see the hamster. The smile was for his supposition—supposition being
the brother of expectation. A rich man could decide to become a ranger; after all, *he* had.

Well, maybe not technically. He hadn't been sitting on
a fat wallet when he'd actually applied to join up. But he
had been a rich man for a while not too long before that.
The heavy cees had been gained from smuggling and other

illegal activities during the days when he broke laws instead of enforcing them. He had pissed the money away, because it hadn't mattered. He had been pretty good at it, smuggling. He could have made another fortune easily enough, retired and enjoyed a long and healthy life spending it, too. Instead, he had joined the rangers. At the time, he told himself it was because he wanted to raise hell legally, to be able to kick ass and maybe have his grandfather who'd raised him smile at him from the Great Beyond instead of shaking his spiritual head in disgust. His grandfather had been a ranger and had always hoped Cinch would do the same, though he'd never said so aloud.

But the real reason he'd gone into the service was because he was looking for something. He wasn't really sure what it was at the time, and since, he'd thought it was just doing the job, doing it well, but now he wasn't sure of that, either.

Was it being part of the solution and not part of the problem? Was it helping those who needed it? That had been enough for a long time.

Cinch made a turn and was confronted with the tail of a traffic jam. He saw the problem, less than half a block ahead. A minor collision at an intersection, two vehicles involved, nobody hurt to judge from the yelling he could hear even this far away. Civilization and its discontents. It made him wish he were back in the jungle with the *majivu*. And Chayne, married or not. There was a woman he wanted to explore a little more.

Unable to move, forward or backward for the traffic now piling up behind him, Cinch considered the question of his desires again.

For years, he'd been a ranger. Not the best but not the worst one, either. He'd done the work, kept it clean, applied the law when it was fair, reached for the intent and applied that when the law wasn't right. But there was still something missing.

He'd kept himself clear of involvement, personal involvement, for most of those years. Do the job, move on. Don't let the people get too close, don't put down any roots, don't get attached. When you skyed from world to world, you had to be like a flyweed or a shark—keep swimming or you'd sink.

But now and then, one of the worlds called. And at the most unlikely times and in the most unattractive—at least on the surface—of places. For some reason, something in Cinch awoke and he wanted to be a part of where he was at the moment, wanted to be involved, not just an outsider passing through.

Like back there in the jungle.

An objective ranger would not have gone with O'thea to shoot it out with an unknown force, like they had at that village. An objective ranger would have gathered more evidence before leaping onto the platform where O'thea and Zarant stood with the natives against what they saw as evil. If you took a side, then you tended to look for things to support that side. True, he hadn't liked the governor when they'd met and first impressions were hard to get past; still, he'd gotten past them before. Problem was, when you made a snap judgment based on instinct, you could be wrong. That you weren't most of the time only made it worse, because then you began to trust yourself. Point-shooting was fast and accurate, but only at close range. Outside of a few meters, you had better take your time and aim or you could miss and find yourself in shit up to the eyebrows.

A pair of uniformed local cops rolled past on two-wheeled fuel-cell cycles, threaded their way around the stopped carts and vans and trucks toward the accident.

Yeah, his intuition looked as if it were going to be right one more time: the governor was dirty and the so-called cutthroats were anything but; still, what did it mean? Was it that he would rather stay here and run around in the bush than finish his business and move on? Space to the next planet, right the wrongs, do what rangers had always done?

Maybe. Maybe that was what he had been missing all these years. A sense of place, of being part of a solution where people knew him as Cinch Carston, neighbor, friend, husband, father, and not just as "the ranger."

And if that were true, what was he going to do about it?

The shower and clean clothes helped. He strapped his gunbelt on, adjusted it, looked at himself in the mirror in his cabin. He was never again going to be one of those crisp and shiny young men fresh out of the academy—hell, he'd never been one in the first place. But he looked fit and professional enough.

The drive to the hotel was uneventful, and if he were being followed manually, he couldn't spot the tail.

The hotel was plush, squat and spread out. Workers wore powder blue jumpsuits and smiled mechanically at him as he walked toward the hamster's suite. Yeah, a suite.

A computer queried him at the door and presumably announced him to the IAL. A minute passed. Guy could be in the shower, so Cinch gave him that. But when the second minute began, he turned and started down the hall.

The door opened behind him before he got three meters.

"Ranger Carston," a smooth voice full of authority said. It was not a question.

Cinch turned and looked at the man. He was tall, but not overly so. His black hair was streaked with gray, mostly at the temples, and he had smile lines bracketing his eyes, though he was not smiling now. He wore a muted and expensive gray-on-gray silk two-piece suit and molded slippers. If he had a gun on, it was concealed too well for Cinch to spot it.

"Come in."

The man turned and walked back into the room without waiting to see if Cinch was following. No greeting, no "How are you?" no "Nice weather we're having." Obvi-

ously someone who was used to being obeyed when he issued an order.

Cinch followed the man into the room.

A skylight allowed brightness but not heat into the
place. Oil paintings hung on the walls, a wooden baby
grand piano or a fair imitation of one stood in a corner behind a couch covered with smooth gray leather, or a good
imitation of that. A Persian-style carpet done in blues and
whites lay over a nubby gray carpet. There was a wet bar
against the far wall, a holoproj unit inset into a wall and
a wireless keyboard on a small antique table next to the
couch. A wallet lay on the table next to the keyboard,
along with a keycard and a few coins.

Probably worth a week of Cinch's pay per night to stay
here, not including tips, he figured.

"Sit," the IAL ordered. "Drink?" Still no smile and the
offer hardly seemed serious.

"No, thanks."

The man shrugged and moved to the bar, mixed himself
something from three bottles, triggered the glass's cooler.
Cinch watched the performance, saw the glass frost. He
was aware that the IAL was taking his time and keeping
him waiting. Demonstrating who was in charge.

Technically, the IAL had no jurisdiction here. A ranger
on-site was in charge of an investigation unless officially
relieved of duty. An IAL could do that, but only under
fairly stringent circumstances—if he couldn't prove dere-
liction of duty or outright criminal activity on the field officer's part, it would be worth a nasty reprimand when it
all shook out. So IALs generally didn't downtime somebody unless they had plenty to back it up. They could ad-
vise, but not order. Cinch wasn't too worried—he hadn't
fucked up or done anything illegal. Well, not that the hamster could prove, anyway.

"It has come to our attention since our arrival that there
are certain . . . irregularities with regard to your investigation."

Cinch kept his face as neutral as he could. If the hamster wanted to play it cool and official, fine. He had no patience with assholes.

"I would like to see your identification," Cinch said, "sir."

"Excuse me?"

"Procedure. What would IAL think of me if I failed to properly identify someone representing himself as an investigator?" Cinch gave him a quick fake smile, making no effort to disguise the insincerity of it.

The man's face clouded, but he returned the smile with one of his own, every bit as false as Cinch's. "Of course." He moved to the table, picked up the wallet, tossed it at Cinch.

He caught the wallet easily, opened it and saw the ID card. It looked real enough. He had a scanner on his belt and he pulled it and passed it over the card. "If I might use your keyboard?"

The hamster sighed and nodded at the table.

Cinch plugged the scanner into the socket on the keyboard, tapped in a request. The air lit over the holoproj as the hotel's computer came online. Slats appeared and a holograph of the IAL appeared and did a slow revolution. Superficially, the image of Sedih Peran was a match to the one sneering over his drink, here in the flesh.

Cinch typed a code and the computer went through a fast scan and matched the card with the numbers. Appeared to be a valid ID.

He nodded and tossed the wallet back to the man.

Peran, drink in hand, fumbled the catch. The wallet bounced off his hand and back toward Cinch. Several items spilled from it onto the expensive rug. Cinch didn't offer to retrieve them, but he got a look as Peran moved to do so. A beat-up holo of a woman and two children. A folded document, official ranger stuff, to judge from the design and color of the border. What looked like a starship hardcopy ticket.

Peran stuffed the items back into the wallet and put it back on the table. "Satisfied?"

Cinch gave him another edition of the fake smile.

"As I said, there seem to be certain irregularities, about which we need to speak."

Cinch waited. He wasn't going to play the hamster's game. If he had something to say, let him say it.

The silence stretched. Finally, Peran broke it.

"Suppose you give me a report on your activities since arriving here?"

"Suppose I don't. If you have specifics you would like to address, Inspector, then address them. Otherwise, you are wasting my time."

Once again the clouds passed across Peran's face.

"We are given to understand that you have been in contact with a group considered dangerous and subversive by the local government."

"As part of my investigation, yes."

"Our sources indicate that you have been aiding these subversives in their activities."

That surprised Cinch, but he didn't let it show. "Are you accusing me of criminal activity, Inspector?"

"Not just yet, ranger. I am interested in your response to the . . . allegations."

"You have vid or vox recordings of my supposedly subversive activities? Witnesses?"

"What I have or don't have will come to the attention of the proper authorities in due course, Carston. It would be better for you to tell me what you have done and what you are doing before I make my report."

Cinch stared at the man. He was every centimeter the officious IAL officer, smug, snide, righteous. Giving him a chance to come clean, spill the truth, to deflect at least some of the hammer's force when it fell. So that he would merely be flattened and not crushed. It was IAL to the nth degree.

And it was wrong.

He couldn't have said exactly what it was that was wrong about Peran, but he'd played enough poker for a lot of years and this smelled like a bluff. Whatever else was going on, Peran wasn't planning to have Cinch slammed with charges. He would bet his retirement on that.

And if that was so, what *was* going on here?

In his tub, soaking, Lavan got the call from Vita.

"I found the camp."

"You sure?"

"Sure enough. Humans and gray monkeys together. What else could it be?"

"Take it out."

"Before the sun sets it will be history."

"Good. Call me when it's done."

"It's already done. They just don't know it yet."

"Don't be so sure. You've thought so before."

"A few men with hunting rifles and some unarmed animals? Come on. It's past tense, I'm telling you."

"Tell me again afterward."

"Discommit, then. I'll get back to you."

Lavan smiled. Finally—finally!—things really were going his way. The ranger was tied up, the major impediment was about to be removed. He might as well call in the corporations and start serious negotiations. But just in case, he would wait until he had Zarant's and maybe O'thea's heads on a platter, and the ranger chasing his tail or also beyond causing him any more concern.

Life wasn't always simple but if you paid attention you could outsmart it. When he'd been in university, he'd been a fairly good student. And why not? He was bright if somewhat indifferent—some called him lazy—and he managed to skate through most of his courses without having to work too hard. There was a time when he needed a grade and didn't have time to study for it and he'd figured out a way into the professor's personal computer for the answers. Now there were people who would have thought that lazy, if anybody had ever found out. But it had actually taken more brains and skill to break into the file than studying for the damned exam would have taken. Less time, sure, but it wasn't as if he hadn't been smart enough to pass the test if he had studied. That was the thing. It wasn't cheating if you could do it anyway.

That was how he looked at it. And it made perfect sense to him.

# chapter 15

"I'll get back to you," Cinch told Peran.

"You'll—" The man shut up, and his frown blossomed. "Listen, Carston, you're in a lot of trouble—"

"Maybe so," Cinch cut in. "But it's my neck on the block, isn't it?" He turned to leave.

"You don't want to do this," Peran said. "Look, you tell me what's going on, what your side of all this is. Maybe I can save you some grief. You need to work with me here. No man is an island, entire of itself."

If Cinch hadn't already turned around, Peran might have seen the puzzled expression on his face. No man is an island? A hamster, quoting John Donne? Sure, the man could have a classical education, given that he was probably rich, but the line rang out as if delivered in a stage play or an entcom vid. Something was not right about that. And there seemed to be a measure of something else in his voice, a kind of desperation. As if he had to find out what Cinch knew. As if that were more important than what he might have done against regs.

"I've got something to check out, Inspector," Cinch said, still heading for the door. "I'll get back to you with everything you want to know as soon as I finish. You, ah, reminded me of something that can't wait."

"Carston—!"

Yes, desperate, no doubt of it.

Cinch exited the suite and hurried down the hall. A thought occurred to him. Had Lavan bought himself an IAL agent? Bribed the man somehow? Rangers were human or pretty close to it, most of them, and if enough money got flashed, they could be tempted. IAL went where it wanted, chose field ops at random and threw surprise inspections. Peran would have checked in with the local government as a courtesy when he arrived. Maybe Lavan had seen an opportunity and jumped on it. What better way to find out what Cinch knew and was up to than to have it delivered to a tame inspector?

Cinch left the hotel, walked into the hot afternoon. Clouds had built to the west and the first bits of scud presaged the coming thunderstorm.

Another thought arose. Wasn't it a big coincidence that an IAL just happened to arrive here in time to debrief Cinch after his visit to the jungle?

Yeah. A real big coincidence.

What if IAL hamster Sedih Peran weren't a ranger at all?

That made him pause in his march toward his ATV. Would Lavan have gone to all that trouble, to hire somebody to impersonate an IAL, just to find out what he knew?

If so, that was a major bit of evidence, could Cinch prove it. Which, he knew, would be possible. All he had to do was point his pistol at Peran, threaten to pull the trigger, and convince him that he meant it. Not that he would shoot the man, but he was a fair poker player himself. Or he could plant a bug of his own and listen. If Peran was Lavan's lapdog, sooner or later he would bark for his master.

Yes. It made a certain kind of sense. He could be wrong, Peran might be exactly what he represented himself to be. And if that were the case, Hacksaw's slapping his wrist and fining him a beer sure wasn't going to satisfy IAL, did Cinch threaten to shoot one of their own. They would scream high, loud, and repeatedly for his head and probably would get it.

Ah, well. Life was full of risks.

Meanwhile, he had a job to do.

Cinch parked the ATV outside a shopping center and went to find a public com. He didn't want to use his personal unit, even though he had a pretty good eavesdrop-stop scrambler connected to the device. Out in the jungle when it was only his problem, he would trust it. Here, where one of Zarant's agents might be put at risk, he wouldn't risk that somebody might scan his transmission and decode it. They wouldn't be able to check all public coms all the time, and he would connect his scrambler to whichever unit he picked to be certain. Not absolute proof, but unlikely anybody would run it down.

When he was sure nobody was doing a visual surveillance, Cinch found a pay com in a nook outside a fresher. He connected his scrambler and punched in the memorized number Zarant had given him.

"Yes?"

The voice that answered was electronically altered, changed into a chipvox's metallic drone. It was deepened enough so he couldn't tell whether the speaker was young or old, male or female.

Cinch's scrambler also modified his voice into something unrecognizable. "A friend told me to call you."

"I've been expecting you," the eerie bass drone came back.

"I need some information."

"Ask."

"First, do you know anything about an IAL ranger, Sedih Peran, who showed up here? Second, can you get me any hard copy or recordings of interesting conversations between somebody very high in authority here and somebody he shouldn't be talking to? Third, are there any computer files of interest to somebody looking for corruption in high circles?"

Cinch looked around, saw a little boy and his mother— had to be, they looked so much alike—heading toward the fresher, nobody else nearby. He didn't make eye contact with them.

"I know that the man called Peran left a message for you, nothing else about him. I'm working on collecting data, but they are hard to come by and even harder to remove unobtrusively. I know of certain files but the security codes protecting them are combinations of vox, retina patterns, and passwords and I can't get to them. I'll try to find out more about Peran and there's a good chance I can get some data compiled soon. Without an expert computer rascal, I can't free the files, but I know they exist."

Cinch nodded unseen at the speaker. Not great, but better than he'd expected. If it got to the legal warrant stage and they were quick enough to grab stuff before it got deleted, that would be helpful. Of course, he needed more evidence now to get that far.

"I'll call you back later," Cinch said.

He clicked the com off. Well. Every little bit helps.

The mother and son emerged from the fresher and walked away. Cinch, suddenly hungry, went to find a place to eat.

He was halfway through some kind of cheese and soypro burger when his com chimed.

"Carston," he said.

"Ranger, you know who this is."

It was Zarant's voice. He couldn't believe the man had called him.

"Don't worry about them tracing this," he said. His voice was grim. "We aren't where we were. Vita's thugs showed up and attacked us. We lost ten people, four of ours, six of the *majivu*. I'm . . . in transit at the moment."

*Jesus.*

"They weren't expecting the *majivu* to be armed. Those toys I showed you worked well enough. Vita lost eighteen of his thugs."

*It must have been pretty brutal,* Cinch thought.

"And some of ours are missing. Including Chayne."

The bite of soypro went dead in his mouth. Cinch swallowed mechanically and nearly choked on the suddenly tasteless clump.

"Hiding out?"

"Or captured," Zarant said. "I've got to go, I just wanted to let you know. I'll be in touch."

Cinch stared at the food on the paper plate. *Damn.*

"I've got good news and bad news," Vita said.

Lavan shook his head at the com. He leaned forward in his chair. He was alone in the office. "Somehow I knew it wasn't all going to be good news. Spill it."

"We wiped out most of the camp. A few got away."

Lavan nodded to himself. "That's not so bad."

"I had eighteen troopers killed, five others wounded seriously."

"So what? That's still not so bad, given the result. Hired guns are cheap."

"Zarant and O'thea were among the escapees."

"Shit."

"Yeah. And most of my troops were hit with poisoned darts. The fucking gray men are using blowguns."

"What? They're supposed to be pacifists, fruit and vegetable eaters!"

"One of my fems took a dart in the throat from a good fifty meters away. Little monkey darted from behind a tree, shot her, and was gone before we could blast his ass. They ain't pacifists no more and they melt into the shadows like ghosts."

"But you said you got most of them."

"Yeah. We, uh, did. But a few of them got away. And there are others out in the bush, you know."

Lavan shook his head. Vita was lying. The attack had been less than the success he was pretending it was. Dammit!

"We're on the trail," Vita said. "I'll let you know when we catch the rest of them." Then he cut the com before Lavan could say anything else.

The com buzzed again almost immediately.

"What now?"

It was the Actor.

"Did you download the ranger?"

"Not exactly."

Lavan wanted to scream. "What exactly does that mean?"

"He came by. We established contact but he had some business to take care of before we got too far along. He'll be coming back later to talk."

"Is he going to tell you what he knows?"

"Of course," the Actor said, his voice as smooth as lube on plate glass. "Everything."

"When?"

There was a slight pause before the Actor oozed in to fill it. Lavan's stomach lurched.

"We didn't set up a specific time, but soon."

"How soon? Today? Tonight? Tomorrow?"

"It wasn't in my character to ask. The guy is fooled—I know what I'm doing here—trust me."

The belly lurch Lavan felt expanded into the feeling of free-fall from a great height. Trust the Actor? Right, as high as he could levitate by spinning his dick one-handed like a propeller. He said, "Listen, you'd better be right about this. If you don't get what I need, the curtain is going to fall on your act permanently."

"Don't worry. I've got it under control."

They discommed.

Lavan stood and paced back and forth in the office. This was really beginning to piss him off. He had other duties, things which must be attended to if he were going to keep the planet's functions on an even keel long enough to profit from it. He couldn't afford to be sitting around, just waiting. He had to attend to his regular duties, but the thought of doing so irritated him. He wanted this business over with, done, finished. It was beginning to look as if the only way for that to happen would be if he went out and did it himself.

The inner door opened and Pakita stuck her head into the office. "Anything I can do for you, Governor?"

"No," he said, his voice sharp. "Not now."

"Excuse *me,*" she said. She shut the door, held the close button down long enough so the motors whined in protest before she finally spared them.

Great. Now his secretary was mad at him. Just what he needed.

Why was his life so much harder than everybody else's?

The memory of those exams at university came back to him. Once he had discovered that he could get into one professor's computer, then what was the point in breaking his balls to study other material? What worked for one would work for others.

Had certainly worked for others.

Until the unfortunate day when he tripped a safety one particularly paranoid instructor left in a simple exam answer program. Then there were devils to pay.

Fortunately, he hadn't been so stupid as to use his own computer or ID to do his electronic sneakery, so the list of possible information thieves was a long one. There were hundreds of students enrolled in that particular woman's classes and, except for a very few, none who would turn down answers to a major test if it were offered to them. They knew somebody had broken in and stolen the answers, but they did not know it was Lavan.

Neither had he been so stupid as to use previously gained information to give himself anything like a perfect score. He supposed there were idiots who might do that, just as there were fools who sometimes plagiarized material and offered it up without reading it. How embarrassing it must be to be called in to explain something as simple as an embedded copyright code in the middle of one's term file.

No, he'd been careful. Not so careful he managed to miss the safety, but enough so they couldn't stencil the crime on him.

Alas, that meant he had to go back to real work for a time, though. Alerted to the possibility, most of the university instructors encrypted their files and festooned them with a thick ring of new safeties. Not that they couldn't be defeated—a lock invented by one man could be opened by a key invented by another—but it was a matter of effort versus results. There came a point of diminishing returns. True, he could figure out a way to bypass the wards, if he worked hard enough, but it was easier to return to actually studying. The thrill of winning only went so far to balance the energy it took to do so.

For the balance of his career in university, Lavan was a solid if not brilliant student who earned his scores honestly. No one ever suspected him; or, if they did, they never spoke of it to him.

That was then. This was now.

He sighed. It was true that the best-laid plans did often have glitches that had to be addressed.

Fortunately, he was seldom, if ever, at a total loss for variations on a theme. If you had enough keys, one of them would eventually fit.

LONE STAR

chapter 16

On the way back to his room, Cinch worried about Chayne. Sure, she was an adult, had military training, and from their shared experiences, was able to take care of herself as well as anybody. But she could have been wounded in the fight. Or taken prisoner. The notion bothered him more than it should. Then again, he was a man first, a ranger second. He had made love with Chayne, shared himself with her as she had with him, and he didn't want to see anything happen to her. Not that there was a lot he could do about it just now. It was a big jungle and if Zarant hadn't been able to find his wife, Cinch doubted that he was going to stroll through the brush and happen across her. No, for that, he'd have to sit tight and wait.

The ATV had an entcom radio set installed in it. He hadn't used it yet, but as the traffic piled up and slowed his pace, Cinch tapped the control panel and lit the radio. He scanned the channels. There were three or four different kinds of music, ranging from ancient classical stuff like Beatles, to *a cappella* choirs doing vox-scat, to post-ultra-retro-bash bands that sounded less like music and more like somebody murdering a room full of synthesizers with an ax.

**114**

There was also a news flash and Cinch scanned it just in time to hear the announcer promo a weather 'cast.

He grinned. That ought to be a really tough job in this area. The weather? Hot, with a ninety percent chance of afternoon thundershowers. Same tomorrow. And the day after that.

Sure enough, when a female voice designed to stiffen erectile tissue came on, that was the forecast. Except for an addition:

"And in the worldpix, Oceanic climesats reveal that tropical storm *Arracher,* eight hundred kilometers southwest of Lesser Baharis, has been upgraded to the first *wembemvua* of the season. As of noon today Northwestern Standard Time, *Arracher* was at Class Three force, with sustained winds of 150 klicks near the center; however, forecasters are predicting that the razor storm will continue on a northeasterly track for the next sixty to eighty hours, thus gathering strength as it passes through the Sticky Doldrums. *Arracher* is expected to achieve Class Two status by first landfall and, according to Dr. Pym ula Griun, chief meteorologist at the WWS, could possible reach Class One."

A man's deep and gravelly voice replaced the woman's:

"The Doldrums are two degrees hotter right now than they were a year ago; that adds up when you're talking about something this big. Our models can't give us a track more than three days ahead, but if it clears the islands and keeps driving northeast, it could twirl itself up to a C-1 by the time it reaches the continent. If it reaches the continent."

The woman came back on the radio. "Thank you Dr. Griun. A *wembemvua* alert has been issued to residents of the Baharis Chain from Eékor Island to Kepala North."

Cinch tuned out the rest of the 'cast. He should probably look at a map again. He remembered only vaguely the geography of the equatorial region. It was a few thousand klicks from here as he recalled. A lot could happen with a hurricane—they were unpredictable. He had been on Imbobay's World a few years earlier and with millions of others had watched fascinated as a hurricane danced around in lazy spirals for almost two weeks in the local gulf before it decided to come ashore. It made one shallow pass over land, hit the ridge of an unseasonable high-pressure area, then circled back out to sea and retreated along its original track and died. Weather control was still in early childhood on most worlds, and on tropical planets, the theory was always beyond the practice.

He reached his cabin, finally, left the ATV, and walked to the door. There were a dozen things he could be doing to further his investigation and he should be doing them. But right at this moment, he was tired. He needed a fresh perspective. He checked the inside of the place, locked the door, set his portable alarm to watch both the front and back doors, and fell onto the bed.

He thought he might be too tired to sleep.

He was wrong.

His com chimed and he came awake, groggy for an instant before he realized where he was and what the noise meant.

"This is Carston."

"Hold it for a second, my vox IDer is acting up."

Cinch recognized the speaker as the spy. The voice was computer-altered but the cadence was the same as before.

"Okay, ID shows clear. You know who this is?"

"Yeah."

"The engine on your ATV needs attention. Go to the service station west of your cabin and have it looked at."

The com phased off.

Cinch shook his head, trying to clear it. How long had he been asleep?

According to his chrono, almost three hours. He was still fuzzy, but he knew he would feel better for the nap in a few minutes.

He went to the fresher, used it, washed his face. He checked his belt gear, looked around, then went to the ATV.

The service station had pumps for chemical fuel, chargers for electrical batteries, and fuel-cell activators, all lined up in neat rows. There were four other vehicles being fueled or serviced when he drove in.

A muscular man in a stained coverall approached the ATV. He wiped his hands on a lube-stained red rag and smiled at Cinch. "What can I do for you?"

"Cart seems to be running a little ragged," Cinch said, playing his part.

"Hmm. Pop the cowling and let's have a look."

Cinch thumbed the engine cover's control and the cover raised hydraulically and split, exposing the engine. The man in the coverall bent and looked underneath. He fiddled with various controls and adjusted them.

"Put 'er online."

Cinch started the engine.

The man leaned back and listened for a few seconds, then reached in with the oiled rag and did something Cinch couldn't quite see.

"I think that's got it," the man said, coming around to look at Cinch where he still sat in the control seat. "Charger belt was a little slack. It shouldn't give you any more trouble."

"Thanks. What do I owe you?"

"Ah, no problem. Take 'er easy."

He turned and walked away.

Cinch pulled out of the station and drove back in the general direction of his cabin. Anybody listening to the bug still operating in the ATV would probably think nothing of the encounter. As he glanced into the rear viewer at the station behind him, he saw the man who'd checked his engine walk to a scooter and mount it, then drive off in the opposite direction.

Cinch grinned. The guy probably didn't even work there. Sharp.

Letting whoever had him under electronic surveillance keep tabs on him had its good points but right now was not one of them. He pulled his inducer from his belt and set it to draw power from the ATV's main battery. The bug hidden and listening in the frame was about to get a surprise.

Cinch clicked the inducer.

The bug got a jolt of energy it couldn't possibly handle and its circuitry got fried.

They could be eyeballing him or footprinting him from a spysat, so Cinch found a parking garage next to a shopping center and pulled in. Aerial surveillance just went away and it only took him a couple of levels to realize nobody was tailing him.

He parked the cart, opened the cowling, and got out. It only took a second to spot the tiny case stuck to the inside of the cowling. He pulled the plastic box—it was about the size of pistol magazine—free and slipped it into his pocket. He shut the engine cover quickly. Still nobody around.

He was hungry again, so he walked to the shopping center to which the parking garage had been appended and looked for a restaurant. He found a place specializing in seafood. It was set up like a cafeteria: there was a line of plastic food displays from which to choose, no human servers. Pick a display and give the number to the friendly computer. He ordered a house special, some local freshwater fish that looked something like catfish. While he was waiting for the food to be delivered on a tray through a slot at the end of the line, he casually pulled the plastic box from his pocket and opened it. Inside was a high-density stack-carb infoball. The ball gleamed dully under the cafeteria's lights. Cinch dropped the ball back into the case and returned it to his pocket.

He found a seat, opened the self-heating tray, enjoyed

the aroma of the steaming fish. It smelled better than it looked, and a moment later, proved to look better than it tasted. He'd never been what anybody would call a gourmet cook—he ate prepared food most of the time. In his job, with all the travel it entailed, that was to be expected. And no matter how good the restaurant, there was something about home-cooked food that always seemed more satisfying.

Cinch grinned as he ate a bite of the fish. It wasn't *that* bad. Food was strange. When he'd been a kid, his grandfather had introduced him to soydogs. This was a sealed tube of soypro inside a bun, covered with a meat and bean concoction called chili, topped with a slice of cheese and chopped onions. He'd loved the taste of those sandwiches when he'd been eight. Years later, when he was on his own, he tried to make them at home. They never tasted quite right. From talking to other people and the reading he did, he understood that taste buds changed as a man aged and for a time, he thought that was the reason the soydogs he made at home weren't as good as he remembered. Then one day he was talking to a cook who'd learned his trade in jail. The slam chef said, "Hell, ranger, it's the ingredients. You ain't cheap enough."

Cinch hadn't understood.

"Look, you buy a chili-cheese-soydog at a hole-in-the-wall stand, they're gonna use stale bread, processed crap that is only a distant cousin to real cheese, the lowest grade of soypro for the dog, and freeze-dried and reconstituted chili. Whole thing'll cost 'em a pentel, maybe, and they peddle it for two cees. They use whole grain bread, #1 soypro or aged cheese, it'll cost 'em maybe a quarter. Be a lot healthier to eat, but it wouldn't be the same animal, you hear what I'm sayin'? What you remember is a *crappy* soydog. You make it with those ingredients, it'll taste just like it did when you were a kid."

Cinch hadn't really believed him, but when he'd given it a try, the cook had been right. And despite the knowledge that the result was junk, he continued to make them that way. And loved every bite.

The fish wasn't that bad. Maybe it was made better by hoping what was on the infoball would be what he needed to put Governor Lavan away for a long time . . .

Lavan had no patience for the drudgery of government today. He thumbed forms and made them official, listened to complaining politicians and citizens with enough clout to get a com through or even a personal visit. He smiled, nodded, made soothing noises, made promises he could not possibly keep even if it had been his intention to do so. None of it mattered, or it wouldn't in a few weeks. He would be gone, leaving all this behind him. Sure, being the headman was fun, but not as much as living for a long, long time with lots of money. If he wanted to dabble in politics again in a few years, certainly a thick stack of cees wouldn't hurt. Make that leap when he got to it.

Yes, *when*. The Actor seemed confident about his part and he hadn't flopped before. Vita and his goons were out in the jungle and they had managed a limited success. All was hardly lost.

He sighed as Pakita opened the door and showed another of the local important men into the inner office. He had to stop worrying so much—it wasn't doing any good and it only made him feel bad.

He smiled at the man.

"Ah, M. Tolst. How good it is to see you again! How can I be of service?"

The man nodded at Lavan, as if the respect were valid and as if he had earned it. Pah. Soon he would be out of this drudgery.

In his room, after a careful search for hidden eyes or ears, Cinch used his personal flatscreen to upload the files in the infoball and scan them.

There was some pretty good stuff here. Dates, names,

deals. A couple of files that were transcribed conversations of recordings that weren't on the ball itself but were referenced as if the writer had them.

Unfortunately, most of the shady stuff was minor, local crime, and not something with which the rangers would ordinarily concern themselves. The kind of thing he wanted was only hinted at, and when it was, the evidence was more circumstantial than hard.

Too bad.

But something was better than nothing. At the very least, having places to look might save some work. And Cinch guessed that the spy would be able to get more. It would be nice to have it all handed to him, but he never depended on that. A lot of times, it seemed to work out that about the time he thought he had everything locked down, knew exactly what was going on, he got a surprise. He supposed he ought to expect the unexpected by now but that was the problem—if you could, then it wouldn't be . . .

Ah, well. One foot in front of the other and see what happened when it happened. The essence of Zen, and, he supposed, ranger work, too.

chapter 17

Once again Cinch was jolted from sleep by the com.

This time it was Sedih Peran. He hadn't decided exactly how he was going to play it, but he was sure he didn't trust the man. If he was a genuine and honest IAL, then any scat Cinch fed him would come back to haunt him later. He figured he could live with that. The worst thing they could do would be to throw him out of the rangers; here lately, that didn't seem so awful. When you started looking around a place with the idea of maybe settling there someday, maybe it was time to break the circuit and exit gracefully. He'd had these kinds of thoughts before. There was a woman on Roget he wanted to contact if he ever got serious about pulling the plug and leaving the rangers. He wondered how she would get along with O'thea and Zarant—

"Ranger?"

Cinch brought himself back to the present. All right. If Peran here wasn't legit, then whatever he could do to screw up the man's agenda was what he ought to do, until he found out whom he was really working for.

"Sorry. I'll meet you at your room in half an hour," Cinch said. "And fill you in on everything."

* * *

Pakita said, "You have two calls cycling on your private number."

Lavan nodded at her. "Close the door on your way out."

He waited until she was gone then scanned the callers' IDs. One was the Actor; the second was listed as IGM. And calling from a local hotel.

Jesus and Buddha in a Singalese Whorehouse! Intergalactic Mining. The corporation that was going to make him super-rich.

The governor reached for the connect plate, then stopped. The Actor could certainly wait until hell sold liquid oxy drinks to the sinners; the IGM people were his ticket to forever. Then again, he didn't want to seem too eager, now did he? There were other companies that would be happy to own a quarter of a continent of extremely valuable mineral deposits, along with the perfectly legal right to strip or crater or pit mine it right down to the molten core, if that's what they wanted. And he was the governor, wasn't he? Let them cycle for a few minutes. One of the cardinal rules of politics or business was: Never let them see you sweat, never let them hear you pant.

"Yes?" he said to the Actor.

"Our little bird is flying over to tell all."

"Good. About fucking time. Call me back when you're finished."

"Of course."

A week ago, he would have grinned, but with all the crap falling from the sky lately, Lavan was now a little more cautious in his belief and his expectation. When he knew what the ranger knew, then he'd allow himself to relax and feel a little better. Meanwhile, the corporation's rep was still cycling offline . . .

"Governor Lavan here."

"Ah, Governor." The voice was warm, female, inviting. A secretary or assistant?

"This is Murie Vendle. I'm the Field VP for IGM Real Estate Acquisition."

Lavan waved his hand at his computer and brought his people log online. He quickly scanned the names until he found the IGM file. No "Vendle" on the list.

"I normally speak with M. Trilee," he said.

"Yes, well, M. Trilee has suffered a rather tragic accident. His yacht crashed on Thamebuqtu after being holed by an errant piece of orbital debris. I'm afraid M. Trilee is no longer with us."

*Or anybody else, it sounds like,* Lavan thought.

"I am now handling all major acquisitions for the company," Vendle continued, "and I see that you were scheduled for a meeting to finalize certain contract negotiations in the next few weeks. As it happens, I am on a short stopover on your world on my way to Háult's Planet and I thought we might get together and . . . chat."

*Just happened to be in the neighborhood? Right. And I can walk on water.* But aloud, he put a thick layer of sincerity into his voice as he said, "How delightful. Of course we must get together."

"I trust that the negotiations you began with the late M. Trilee are still of interest to you?"

"Indeed. I have all but wrapped up the package—a few niggling details that still must be attended to, but basically I am ready to speak seriously with IGM."

"Good, good. It would be terrific if we could set things up while I am here; it would save me another trip."

Now he did smile. He knew this kind of game well enough. If IGM wanted his property badly enough—and he was fairly certain they did—M. Vendle would straddle a comet to travel here and meet him, as many times as it took. "My schedule is a bit hectic this afternoon but perhaps we could meet tomorrow? For lunch?"

"Let me see . . . yes, lunch would be fine."

"I'll have a conveyance sent to pick you up. Say, about 1300?"

"Fine. I'm staying at the—"

"—Superb Benson," he finished. "I'll see you tomorrow, then."

He broke the com and pinched his upper lip between his thumb and forefinger. Hmm. So IGM was getting antsy and they'd sent a woman from uplevel to close the deal. Fine by him. It wasn't quite ready to put the ribbon on it yet, but it was close. That they had sneaked an exec onworld and hidden her in the oldest and most exclusive hotel on the planet was something of a surprise. He had a flag on visas bearing IGM imprints and somehow hers had gotten past his security. He supposed anybody with as much money and clout as IGM had could manage such things, but it bothered him nonetheless.

Ah, well. What did it matter? Once the gray apes were gone the deal would fly like a sunship, elegantly and smoothly. A bonded survey team, all quite objective scientists imported from offworld, would go forth and when they failed to find any of the natives, the giant reserve would default to control of the state to do with as the state—meaning "he"—wished. A matter of a month or so for the legalistic eyewash, funds would be transferred, and he would leave this place and not look back. It was a fortunate happenstance that the early settlers had written into the constitution that the duly elected governor had the sole right to dispose of parks, reserves, and other reverted land grant properties as he saw fit, "for the good of the people and the planet."

True, IGM's chop and dig operations would leave raw wounds in the land, gaping holes that would make the bush look like an airless moon pocked by half a million years' worth of big meteors. So what? It was useless jungle otherwise and if a few thousand acres of trees and vines would be wiped out, it wasn't as if half the land mass on the world wasn't covered with more of the same. The many billions IGM spent, for the land, to pay local workers, in taxes, all would be funneled into the local economy; who could complain, except for a few ape kissers and tree huggers? The real beauty of the scheme, of course, was that most of the money IGM paid would indeed go right into the planetary coffers. He wasn't going to steal all that, no way—he wasn't that greedy. Or stupid. But if the former governor got a nice broker's fee that amounted to, well, a *great deal* of money, where was the real harm? Everybody would be better off.

Well. Almost everybody. And who really cared about a few apes and ecofreaks, anyhow? Not him. Not anybody of importance.

Peran tried to look calm, to maintain a facade of fatherly concern, but now that Cinch was looking for it, he was sure he detected a false note among the well-played chords. So as he leaned back and enjoyed a glass of the excellent local beer, Cinch lied through his smile, too.

"And you are convinced that these cutthroats—O'thea and Zarant are the cause of the problems?"

Cinch nodded. "Yeah. I actually spent some time in a secret camp they had, out in the middle of nowhere."

"You have the location?" Too eager there.

"Sorry, no. They blindfolded me going and returning."

"A pity. Go on."

"Well, like I said, I convinced them that I was only investigating as a matter of routine, that they weren't in violation of any galactic laws but that I had to go through the motions."

"Very clever."

"So I saw their operation. Not much to it, a few gray apelike things running around—"

"The *majivu.*"

"Something like that. And they had a couple of crawlers and some small aircraft. Not much in the way of weaponry, and I only saw a couple of dozen humans."

Peran nodded thoughtfully. "Another beer?"

"No, I'm fine. Good stuff." That was the truest thing he'd said since he'd arrived.

"And the local authorities seem honest?" Peran prompted.

Cinch took a sip of the beer. "Far as I can tell. I had some suspicions at first, you know how these frontier worlds are, everybody from the animal control officer up is looking to line his or her pockets with whatever loose cees they can get hold of."

Peran looked at Cinch and nodded sadly. We men of the galaxy, the look said, we know about these things. Too bad, but what can you do? Crooks are everywhere.

"But far as I can tell, the local headman, the governor, he's clean. The way I see it, these bandits are on a tear for some reason; they claim it's political but I figure they're just using that as an excuse to steal. The governor is trying to take care of it and he called us in, but I don't see that it's our problem. They've got police and military here who can handle it."

"Well," Peran said, smiling. "It seems as if you are doing a proper investigation here, ranger. I believe I can say my report will reflect that."

"Hey, thanks. I appreciate it. I'm getting close to pension time, and I don't want anything on my record that'll sour things."

"Not to worry. So, you're done here, is that correct?"

"Yeah, pretty much. I got a couple of interviews I need to get to finish up, kind of, you know, thicken my report a little so it looks as if I covered all the bases, but basically, it's a done deal. I'll stick around a few more days, a week or so, maybe, so the locals won't think we're dropping it without crossing the t's and all, but I'm already checking the shuttle schedules for a hopper to the liner." Cinch looked at Peran and smiled, another men-of-the-galaxy look.

Peran nodded gravely. "I understand. It would be best to observe the proper forms, for appearances. These locals don't understand how thinly spread the rangers truly are, that they cannot come running to us yelling 'Thief!' every time somebody misplaces his wallet, eh?"

Cinch returned Peran's smile. They understood one another.

Lavan laughed aloud as he heard the recording the Actor had delivered to him. He sat in the soak tub, enjoying the heat and aromatic vapors and replayed the recording for the third time. He had been correct in his first assessment of the ranger after all. The man had stumbled into Zarant and O'thea by accident—that was why he'd been at the camp when the troops had attacked—and he was more worried about his pension than he was about any local problems. Perfect.

Lavan reached for a sniffer and inhaled a spray of potent erectant. Pakita would be by later to help him deflate what the chem even now caused to stir and rise.

He giggled. He was clean, the local headman was, that straight from the mouth of the ranger he'd imported to ascertain just that. By 1330 tomorrow he would be moving well along the path to riches. It was, to steal a phrase from the ranger, a done deal.

It had been an up-and-down few days, but finally— finally!—things were up again.

He glanced down at himself under the warm liquid and giggled again. Up. No doubt about it . . .

When Cinch got back to his room, he found that someone had slipped a note under the door. The tiny slip of plastic was folded once and coated in a gritty substance. It was a thermaplique message, he saw. There was a thumbprint stenciled on the outside and from the little V-shaped scar in the middle of it he recognized the print as his own. How had they gotten it?

He shrugged and put his thumb on the print. That would slow the oxidation process by about twenty seconds. If he tried to open the message without matching the print, it would ignite and go up like a magician's flash paper; as it was, he'd have to hurry to read the message because it was going to vanish into flames pretty quick anyhow.

He unfolded the note.

"They've got Chayne O'thea. Call Zarant."

Cinch stared at the message a few seconds too long. The plastic started to heat up. He dropped it; it flared and was gone before it reached the floor.

He was tempted to grab his com and call Zarant right there, but to do so might mess up the careful disinformation performance he'd just put on for Peran. The com would be shielded and scrambled so a listener wouldn't know with whom he spoke or what was said, but for him to go to that trouble might arouse suspicion. Yeah, it might be SOP for field rangers routinely to shield their communications, but he didn't want to give Lavan or his people any reason to suspect him of anything at this point except being stupid.

Time to go and find another shopping mall with a not-too-public com he could use.

Damn. They had Chayne.

Lavan was in his limo being driven to his luncheon appointment with the IGM VP Murie Vendle. He knew she was lovely, even though they had yet to meet—once he knew where she was, he was able to call up her ID stats, which included a good holograph of the woman. Tall, willowy, jet hair worn unfashionably long, very expensive silks in the picture. This meeting might be more beneficial than he had hoped.

The com's chime blew away the fog of his fantasy.

"Yes?"

"I got the bitch," Vita said. He sounded smug enough about it.

"Which bitch might that be?"

"Jesus, Yogen—"

"O'thea?"

"Yep. My troops found her unconscious in the jungle. She musta taken a whack on the head from something; she was less than half a klick from the campsite."

He felt a nice warm glow suffuse him. "Is her condition serious?"

"Nah. She woke up just fine; our medic says a mild concussion, nothing broke."

"Excellent."

"I take it from your question you don't want me to kill her?"

"God, no. She's our key to Zarant. I don't want you to lay a finger on her, no dork and bush, nothing. We'll use her to reel Zarant in. With the two of them out of the picture, the cutthroat alliance will fold faster than a night lily in the sunshine."

"You think Zarant is just gonna walk in and give himself up because we got O'thea?"

"You know, if you'd pay attention once in a while to the information zipping past your nose, you'd realize that Zarant and O'thea are very close. *Personally* close. He might not want to stroll into our hands, but he will want to free his girlfriend. We don't ask him to *surrender;* we just let it be known that we have O'thea in custody and where we've got her. We catch him when he comes to rescue her. You don't tell the mouse that the bait is part of a trap, you just put it out where he can see it and let him take care of that part. Surely even you can figure out a way to set that up?"

There was a pause. Vita, no doubt, was miffed because Lavan was, as usual, way ahead of him. The man wasn't just an idiot, he was a *slow* idiot.

"Yeah," he finally said. "I can rig a trap."

"I thought so. Don't do anything yet. I've got a meeting I have to attend; I'll call you back afterward and we'll discuss the details."

"All right."

Lavan sank back into the cloned-pigskin cushions, pleased. First the ranger, now this. He rubbed his hand over the soft leather, enjoying the feel of it. He was at last rolling on the high road and he intended to keep it that way. It was all a matter of assembling the proper pieces. If you could do that, sooner or later you could push them into the correct shape.

Cinch found another gathering spot for the locals, a multiplex entertainment center featuring wide-angle holoproj entcoms. Some vids needed to be seen and experienced communally, on a large scale, and there were always enough people who would go and pay to see them in a theater instead of viewing them on smaller holoproj units in their own cubes. This particular plex had nine such features currently online, including the classic full-sensorum remake of *Seven Samurai* and the equally classic new holo-noir version of *Darkworld Detective*. The plex was drawing good crowds, and Cinch paid his admission and went into the detective proj. In the darkened theater, he circled through a rear exit and quickly into the nearest fresher. He didn't think anybody was watching him but even if they were, going to pee should seem harmless enough.

The unit was equipped with privacy booths. He entered one, closed the door, and sat on the bidet. He hooked his scrambler to the booth phone, activated it, and made his call.

"I got your message," Cinch said when he heard Zarant answer.

"Vita's men found her," Zarant said. "She was injured in the attack. I don't know how badly. Or where she is."

"Sit tight. Maybe I can find out something here."

"He'll execute her," Zarant said. The angst was heavy in his voice.

"Is your relationship with her common knowledge?"

"Not the formal marriage, no. But that we're together, yeah."

"That might be enough to keep her alive. You're still out in the jungle with your troops. Killing Chayne won't do anything about that."

"If she's hurt, Vita and Lavan are dead men. It might take me a while to set it up, but it would happen."

"I'd guess they know that. She's more useful to them alive than dead. Alive they can use her against you. Dead, they lose any advantage she might give them."

"So, what do you think they'll do?"

"I don't know. Offer some kind of trade. Threats."

"If I find out where she is, I'll move the goddamned planet to get to her."

Cinch thought about that for a second. "I hear you. I'll

see what I can do. Listen, be very circumspect in contacting me from now on. No calls to my personal com; any messages need to be absolutely invisible. I think I've managed to convince Lavan I'm basically harmless. It would be better if he kept believing it."

"All right. But you'll com me if you find out anything?"

"Yes. Stay out of sight."

"Copy that. Discom."

Cinch was tempted to leave and begin snooping but if his subterfuge was going to work, he needed to play it out. He went back in to see the holoproj. It really was a good story.

The headwaiter and wine steward and service boy all hurried in and out of the private room at the Emerald House, where Lavan sat in a four-hundred-year-old carved and not particularly comfortable chair waiting for the IGM VP to arrive. He had already ordered champagne and three wines to accompany the meal after listening to the headwaiter's description of the luncheon. At the Emerald House, you ate what the chef prepared, there were no menus, and if you had to ask what it cost, you couldn't afford it. Today the entrée was a rock limpet and vampire eel sauté, with asparagus and wavy tubers boiled in mustard wine. The limpet and eel would have been swimming in the ocean this same morning and the asparagus and tubers would have been picked within an hour of being served. Asparagus wasn't one of his favorite vegetables; Lavan always hated the way it made his piss smell, but he would eat it and smile doing it. The chef at the Emerald House had been known to fly into a rage which included attacking with a soup ladle anyone who would dare to bring day-old produce, fish, fowl, or meat into his kitchen. If you criticized the food in any way, you were never allowed to eat in the place again, no matter who you were. There were rich men who had made offhand comments about the fish being dry or the meat undercooked and had been banned before they reached the front exit. The chef was also the owner, and himself a wealthy man who could afford to make enemies. The Emerald House was not only the best restaurant in the city or on Mtizito, it had also earned Five Stars in the *Galactica Gourmandia,* one of only a dozen such ratings ever given on any world upon which men thrived and built restaurants.

Lavan wondered just how much money it would take to convince the chef to sell this place and open a new one on whichever world the governor eventually chose to settle on.

Murie Vendle arrived.

She looked better in person than in her holograph. She wore a wispy bodysuit of nearly transparent black silk, with an electrostatic loin wrap of equally wispy white silk artfully draped about her hips to prevent her from being effectively naked. Her nipples were rouged white so that they appeared a pale gray through the bodysuit and her body was superb. Obviously a woman who cared about her appearance and did whatever exercise or surgery necessary to keep it stunning. She knew what she had and wasn't shy about showing it.

Lavan was especially glad he'd reserved a private room at the city's best restaurant for this meeting. He wanted this vision all to himself.

"Governor Lavan, how delightful to meet you."

He smiled, sincerely happy to say the same. "And please," he added, "do call me Yogen."

"Then you must call me Murie." She extended one hand and he took it, bowed, and touched his forehead to her knuckles. Her fingers were cool and when he raised his head, her smile brought forth deep dimples.

Compared to her, Pakita was a cow.

How much money, he wondered, would it take to have this woman quit her job and become his companion?

After dessert—a flaming hot-and-sour sorbet so good it brought tears to his eyes—Lavan sent the headwaiter away with his compliments to the chef. He waited a few minutes, keeping his conversation with Murie superficial, until the chef and owner, Makan Balut, arrived to inquire about the meal.

"Makan, this is Murie Vendle, a friend of mine visiting from offworld. Murie, this is Makan Balut, the greatest chef in the galaxy."

"Ah, madam, a pleasure." Makan bowed low, then looked at the governor. "Your meal was not too displeasing?"

Lavan laughed. "You are a shameless fisherman, Balut. You know very well this meal was, as each time I have dined here, better than the one before. You well know that you could cook gravel and firewood and it would taste better than any food available elsewhere prepared by anyone. The lunch was superb, incomparable, beyond mere words."

"Ah, yes, but—did you like it?"

Lavan and Murie laughed.

"He is right," she said. "I've never had anything so wonderful."

The chef smiled slightly and gave her a military bow. "One tries."

"I don't suppose you will consider my offer?" Lavan said.

This brought a bigger smile from the chef.

To Murie, Lavan said, "I've been trying to buy this place for years. This old rogue won't sell it to me."

"It would be a bargain at any price," Murie said.

The chef turned his gaze and his smile back upon the woman. "I like your friend, Yogen. You must dine here as my guest as long as she is visiting."

"But of course."

After the chef departed, his ego properly stroked, Lavan smiled at Murie. "With the money you'll make on our arrangement, you could afford to buy this place," she said, and laughed. "Actually, you could probably afford to buy a dozen places like this and a town in which to put them.

He nodded. "I plan to make a serious offer. A good cook is a treasure but a chef like this one is beyond price." He paused a second, then continued smoothly. "But now, let us discuss that arrangement between your company and our little world."

"I'd like almost nothing better." She favored him with an erotic smile that stiffened him under his glowsilks. My, my. Surely that was a double entendre?

This could be a most interesting luncheon indeed. If he played this hand right, he could come away a big winner indeed. The money and the woman to help him enjoy it.

He returned her smile.

# chapter 19

The private rooms at the Emerald House were not only very private when the "Do Not Disturb" sign was lit, they were equipped with certain amenities that included, among other things, a pullout bed and access to a private fresher.

When Murie Vendle was finally finished with him nearly two hours after the dessert, Lavan thought briefly that he might also require the use of a wheelchair. When she emerged from the shower, she looked little different than when he had seen her arrive. But he felt as he imagined it would feel to have been hit by a hovertruck moving at speed. Whatever she had spent on her looks, she must have spent that much at least on perfecting her sexual skills. That finger trick with his prostate during the fellatio was particularly exquisite.

Whatever she cost, he was going to have her.

And she was not averse to the idea, either. Corporate life was becoming boring, she said. She was looking to retire.

With the money he would make on the land sale, Lavan knew he would be a rather spectacular catch for someone willing to cater to his wants and needs. Love wasn't a requirement. The hints they dropped to each other postcoitally were not especially oblique. It was obvious that

Murie wanted a wealthy mate and was willing to do whatever it took to find and hold one. Her rise in her current job had been to that end, to position herself next to such a person, male or female. She was, she said, quite adaptable about such things and certainly willing to experiment. He was about to become one of the richest men in the galaxy. An arrangement was not only possible, it was more or less agreed upon without ever being spoken aloud. Money might not buy true happiness, could the poets and sages be believed, but enough of it would certainly allow a man to purchase a counterfeit that would fool most people. With the life-preservation process looming and such a woman as this as a playmate, as well as more money than a busy man could spend on himself in five hundred years of gracious living, Lavan would be hard-pressed to think of anything that would make *him* happier.

Murie left first. She still had her own limo waiting.

The headwaiter smiled at Lavan as he carefully left the private room. "I do hope you enjoyed your meal, Governor."

"Immensely, Joberto. Put a thirty percent gratuity on my bill for yourself and give the steward and the servers twenty percent each."

"You are most generous, sir."

"Not at all. Not at all."

He fell asleep in the back of his limo going back to his office.

"Residents of Eékor Island are breathing a little easier tonight as *Wembemvua Arracher,* now a Class Two storm with sustained winds of 240 kilometers per hour near the center, turned southeast and away from its dangerous track back into the Doldrums early this morning. Chief meteorologist at the WWS, Dr. Pym ula Gruin, says that the razor storm currently poses no threat to land but warns all island inhabitants to remain cautious in case of another shift in the *wembemvua*'s path."

\* \* \*

Sitting in the small restaurant near his cabin, Cinch ate breakfast while listening to the holoproj playing in the background. He glanced at the screen when the weather report came on. Not much to see, the standard shot of tropical palmlike trees blowing in a fierce wind.

He sipped at the not-too-bad coffee and listened to the talking head deliver the end of the report.

He had gone through a hurricane once. He'd only been about nine TS when it happened. He and his grandfather had spaced to Cameron on a fishing trip—the old man was very fond of trolling from the back of a power boat for big game fish. On Cameron, for some odd reason, they named the tropical storms in the western hemisphere after saints in the local religion. A storm called St. Thelma Louise twirled itself into a major hurricane and headed for the port in which he and his grandfather were staying.

"Should we evacuate, Gramps?"

"What for? This building has been here for a hundred years, according to the owner, gone through twenty hurricanes. If it lasted through those, why wouldn't it last through another one? Besides, after it passes, the fish'll be stirred up good and we still have two weeks of vacation left."

Rudy nodded. He didn't see the flaw in his grandfather's reasoning. It was only years later that he understood the logical fallacy.

The local residents had survived several storms in the past decade and those who planned to ride this one out knew to make preparations. Glass and plastic windows were boarded or taped up, loose objects were stored inside or tied down, water and food staples collected. His grandfather bought a pair of alcohol lanterns and two battery-powered lamps, a forty-liter container he filled with water, and enough freeze-dried food to feed them for two weeks if need be. Rudy helped him lug the stuff to their room. They also hauled one of the sheets of fiberplast stacked outside up to their second floor unit, along with the hotel owner's nailgun, and put the thin but nearly unbreakable sheet over the sliding plastic door that led onto the balcony.

"Problem is pressure," Gramps said. "That door looks right out at the sea and the wind will push hard against it, the storm comes this way. It might hold, it might not, but if a branch or some kind of debris should punch a hole in it, then the wind would funnel right through. If the window on the lee side or the door to the hall should pop open, then there'd be a hell of a flow, it might suck the whole balcony right in here with us. We wouldn't want that."

"You think the fiberplast is strong enough?"

"Hell, yes. The rest of the building will go before it does."

Their preparations made, there was little to do in the day or so before the storm started to arrive in force. Gramps had rented a pair of bicycles for them to use in the small coastal town, and as the wind began to pick up, Rudy joined the local children in a game involving the bikes. On the long street that ran directly from the sea to the cluster of municipal buildings, the children would sit on their bikes, hold up a shirt or square of cloth tied to the handlebars, and let the wind blow them along like sailboats. They got going pretty fast—the gusts were hitting 120, 130 klicks—and it still wasn't raining. Going back up the street toward the ocean wasn't so much fun—you had to get off your bike and lean into the gale, pushing hard to make way. The wind flagged your clothes and your hair, made your eyes water, and there was a lot of dust and crap in the air you had to watch out for. One of the children got hit by a roof shingle and it cut his head, but Rudy didn't have any problems and it was as much fun as anything he'd ever done. Being hurled along, blown like leaves by the front of the oncoming storm, was really exciting.

At least until it started to rain. It so happened that the

first fat drops of the storm arrived while Rudy was at the wrong end of the street. If leaning into the now-almost-hurricane-force wind to push his bike was rough, doing it with rain whacking him so hard it felt like gravel was no fun at all. Within seconds he was soaked as the storm splashed down on them like a waterfall. The world went blurry gray, the rain came in almost horizontally. He couldn't see five meters and it took a long time to get back to the hotel. He chained the bike to Gramps's, where it was locked to a metal light post, and made his way dripping into the hotel.

In the hotel bar, they'd left some of the side windows taped but not boarded, and Rudy stood with a dozen other people watching stuff blow past. Gramps sat at the bar drinking rum punch with four or five other men and a few women. At one point a couple of hours into the storm, Gramps and one of the women left for a while, and when they came back, Gramps was grinning real big.

The power went out just after dark, but the hotel had its own generator and the lights came back on after a few seconds. The holoproj had reports on the storm, the center of which was supposed to pass right over the village around midnight.

The winds increased. Before the streetlight across the lot next to the bar went dark, Rudy saw a section of wooden building go past. It was a corner, part of two walls, and it rolled in a kind of lurching tumbleweed way, pieces breaking off as it went by. The wind was blowing at almost three hundred klicks an hour, so the holoproj guy said.

The noises were fascinating. There was a kind of deep rumble all the time from the wind, and the building groaned and creaked. And it sang. Well, more like it howled, *woooo,* the sound rising and falling in pitch so that it seemed almost like a person. After a while, Rudy was sure he could hear words in the moans. It was weird, but it was almost like somebody calling him.

Gramps came over to stand next to him, a drink in his hand.

"That's the storm talking to you like a Siren," he said. "It wants you to come outside. So it can eat you."

Rudy blinked and, for the first time during the hurricane, he was afraid.

Midnight approached and the winds got harder. The building shook, things rattled behind the bar. All the adults had been drinking or smoking stuff and having a pretty good time, but even they got quiet when something screamed and rumbled up above them, shaking the building like a dog after a bath.

"Shit," the owner said. "There goes the goddamned roof."

Then, almost all of a sudden, the wind stopped.

Rudy stared out through the window. His ears popped, like when they flew in the boxcars down from orbit.

"That's the eye, son," Gramps said. "We're in the middle of the storm. Like a whirlpool. Come on, I'll show you something."

Gramps led him to the door. Most of the others also went outside.

It was amazing. Rudy looked up and saw the stars, sharp as laser beams. The air was as clear as he'd ever seen it. Not a cloud above them.

Gramps yawned, pinched his nose, and blew. Popping his ears, Rudy knew from his scuba diving lessons. To equalize pressure.

All around, debris from the storm lay, pieces of buildings, flattened signs, branches, whole trees and bushes uprooted everywhere. The post where Rudy had chained his bike was gone and so were the bikes.

"Come on, we'd better get back inside."

"How come?"

"We're only halfway through, son. In a few minutes, the wind is going to start back up."

Gramps was right. And more amazing than anything to

Rudy was that the wind picked up and started blowing hard very fast. From the other direction.

The next morning, the rain slackened to a drizzle, they went out. The hotel had been a four-story building. Now there were three stories left. The roof and the top floor were just gone. Most of the buildings in the town still stood but almost all of them were damaged in some way. Crews were already at work with saws and servocats, clearing trees and shattered buildings from streets. Boats were thrown upon the shore, some of them upside down. One boat was on the roof of a restaurant near the shore. On the *roof.*

Rudy blinked in amazement. Yesterday this had been a resort town and today it was a wreck. In the way of nine-year-olds, it had been fun for him. But even then he was smart enough to know that a hurricane was nothing to shrug off. This was a big deal, real powerful stuff.

Gramps had been right about the fish, too. Two days later when they went out, Gramps caught the biggest 'cuda anybody around there had ever seen. Almost two and a half meters long and as big around as Rudy was. A Cameron record that held until after Gramps died ...

"More coffee?" the waitress asked.

Cinch blinked. Jesus, he was turning into a doddering old man, spending all his time in the past. "No, thanks. I'm fine."


"All right, here is how I want it to go," Lavan said to Vita.

The redhead paced across from him in one of Madam Yallaroi's suites, this one designed to look like a desert. Even had sand on the floor, though the air was not quite hot enough to be uncomfortable.

"Take O'thea to the police substation at Pos Restant—"

"Christo, Yogen, that's in the middle of nowhere—"

"Shut up, Munga. Of course it's in the middle of nowhere! You want witnesses to a mass execution?"

Vita kicked at the sand, raising a shower of fine white material.

"Put her in a cell. I'll pull the local police out and you replace them with some of your men. No more than are usually on duty there. Hide the rest of your men in the bush where they won't be seen. I will see to it the word gets out where O'thea is, that she'll only be there for a few days until she's transferred to the city for her trial. Zarant will have to move quickly; he won't have time to check things out too closely."

Vita grinned. "Right. I get it. When he comes, we cut him down."

"No. Given how your people shoot and what's happened before, that's exactly what you *don't* do. You let him get into the station. Have your men inside put up a token resistance, don't make it look too easy, we don't want to alert him. Once he is inside with O'thea, you set off the explosives that you will have wired the building with as soon as the local police are gone. We don't take any chances this time. You'll put enough bombs in to turn the place into powder."

Vita shook his head. "Yeah, that'll work. But—what about my men, the ones pretending to be cools? They'll get killed, too."

"So what? You know how much money is at stake here, don't you? They are mercenaries; they knew the job was risky when they signed on."

"Yeah. I guess you're right."

"Of course I'm right. I'm the brains here, Vita. You're the muscle. Let's not forget that."

Vita glared at him, kicked up a little more sand.

Lavan knew he could no longer trust the man. Given the opportunity, Vita would betray him, if he thought he could get away with it—and the money, of course. Lavan wasn't going to let it happen.

The governor smiled. "But let's not dwell on such things. I'll have Colonel Brecht deliver the explosives and detonators to your storehouse in the morning and I'll pull the police by noon. You can wire the building and move O'thea in by tomorrow evening."

Vita nodded sharply, still simmering.

"Look, I know I've been treating you somewhat harshly of late," Lavan said. "I don't want you to think I don't appreciate you. I've just been, well, somewhat nervous about things. You understand."

Vita looked at him warily.

"I've brought you a present."

Vita's eyebrows went up. "A present?"

"Yes." With that, Lavan went to the small case he'd brought and opened it, then turned it around for Vita to see.

Inside was a small oak box not much bigger than a laptop flatscreen. He handed the box—it was heavy—to Vita. The man took it carefully and opened the lid on its cleverly hidden hinges.

Inside the oak box, which was mostly solid wood with two insets carved out by a cutting laser, were a pistol and a spare magazine for it.

Vita's eyes went wide.

"It's a Walther Vasara," he said, his voice full of awe. "A ten millie!"

He removed the gun and held it up almost reverently. It was quite impressive as such things went. The pistol was black-chromed stainless steel with cream-colored grips and a built-in laser and dot scope. It fired ten-millimeter caseless ammunition, small rockets, really, either armor-piercing exuran or explosive-tipped slugs. It was almost the twin of Lavan's personal handgun, a weapon over which Vita had nearly orgasmed when first he had seen it. They were handmade at the Walther factory in Old Deutschland, easily worth a year's salary for a solid, middle-class office worker, and there was a two-year waiting list to obtain one. Lavan had bought this one second-hand, and it had cost more than it would have from the factory because the owner was loath to part with it.

"Is it really for me?"

"Yes. A small gift to show my appreciation for your hard work."

Vita dropped the pistol's magazine by pressing the release button, racked the slide to make certain the chamber was empty, then pointed the weapon at a fake palm tree and pulled the trigger. "Blam!" he said, over the sound of the hammer falling with a *click!*

"Oh, man, thank you, Yogen! Thank you!"

Lavan smiled. Like a child with a new toy. Of course, it was a terrific piece of hardware, and to a man who played with guns, irresistible. He could be sure that Vita would not allow this gift to be out of reach anytime soon. It would ride on his hip or lie next to him while he slept.

It was a shame about the Walther, but it was the cost of this business and it had to be done. While the smooth and buttery grips on Lavan's pistol were genuine cloned curlnose tusk, fine ivory that had been aged for a year before being cut to fit the pistol, those on this handgun were a clever imitation. They were a polymer, cast from sawdust made from the real thing and a special resin mixed with seventy-five grams of Kilatex explosive. Seventy-five grams of Kilatex was enough to reduce an ATV to burning tires and a smoldering hole in the plastcrete under them, or to shatter everything inside a large room into fingernail-sized pieces. Also cast into the gun grips were two tiny RC detonators tuned to a certain narrow radio frequency.

The exact same frequency as the detonators Vita was to place inside the police substation with Chayne O'thea.

Whatever else Vita might be, he was going to cease to be a problem at the same moment that Zarant and O'thea ceased to be problems.

"It's really beautiful, Yogen."

Lavan smiled. Yes. It was beautiful. But he wasn't thinking about the gun itself when he nodded.

# chapter 20

Cinch got a com from Peran on his way back from dinner the next day. He was on foot, strolling through the rain-cooled evening, when his belt unit cheeped for his attention.

"Carston here."

"I thought you might find it interesting to know that one of the cutthroats has been captured," Peran said.

"Really? Who would that be?"

"The ex-colonel, O'thea. Apparently she was taken in a battle a couple of days ago."

Cinch waited. He didn't want to arouse suspicion. And if the man hadn't wanted him to know, he wouldn't have called.

"The governor himself commed me. The authorities are apparently holding her in some backwoods jail, keeping her out of sight until they can arrange for a transfer to the central prison here in the city."

"Good for them," Cinch said.

"Yes, the governor seems quite pleased about it." A beat, then, "You know, you might wish to interview her, for your report."

"I don't think that'll be necessary," Cinch said, trying to

147

keep his voice calm and offhand. "I mean, I'm basically done here, pretty much."

"You're sure? She's being held in a police station jail in some place called Pos Restant. I don't know the local geography but I'm sure the governor would be happy to direct you to wherever it is."

Cinch sucked in a quick breath. They'd just handed him the information Zarant would kill for, all neatly packaged, as easy as that.

Maybe too easy.

Cinch said, "Maybe I'll have the governor's people send me a copy of her statement when they question her. No reason I need to talk to her."

"Well, it's your investigation," Peran said. "Whatever you think is best."

They discommed and Cinch continued his drive toward his cabin.

He was crossing an intersection, the traffic signal in his favor, when a small three-wheeled scooter ran the light and bumped into Cinch's ATV.

He saw it coming and almost avoided it, but it looked as if the idiot driving the scooter swerved to hit him. The collision was slight, no big damage Cinch could see when he stepped out to look. The other driver, a middle-aged woman with gray hair and big eyes, stammered that it was her fault.

"Doesn't look as if it hurt my cart any," Cinch said. "Are you all right?"

She took a pen from her pocket and wrote a name and number on a slip of paper, handed it to him. "My insurance will pay for any damages," she said. "Let's not involve the police, okay?"

Cinch shrugged.

Before he reached his ATV, the woman was in her scooter and zipping away. Other vehicles sounded their horns and drivers started yelling, so Cinch hurried to move his own cart from the intersection.

It wasn't until he was in the ATV and rolling that he realized the slip of paper had folded inside of it a thin sheet of thermaplique plastic.

He grinned. Whoever Zarant's spy was, the guy was clever.

The thumbprint-protected message flared in the cart's disposal tray with a *whoof!* and was gone. What it said was "Stop by the small market next to your cabin and buy a few things."

Cinch parked the ATV next to his cabin and went inside. He waited a few minutes, then left and strolled toward the market, which was only a five-minute walk away.

Inside the small store a couple of other customers prowled the aisles. Cinch picked up a tube of beard depil, a magazine module for the Mtizito edition of *NewsFax,* a liter of beer. He walked to the checkout counter and presented his credit card to the scanner. A clerk pushed his purchases into a paper bag—they still had a lot of timber to use for that on this planet—then returned his card.

As Cinch was leaving, a bearded man entering the store bumped into him, excused himself, and moved past.

The ranger sauntered back to his cabin, went inside, and after a check for monitoring devices, looked inside the paper bag to discover that a fourth item had found its way there. Another infoball.

He slotted the ball in his reader and scanned the files.

One of the folders was full of communications information, logs of calls between the governor and dozens of people on three different codes, including one marked "PC." Private com, maybe?

Cinch read the names. Most of them he didn't recognize. They were identified by com numbers and sometimes company names, any of which would seem to be a legitimate correspondent for the governor of a planet. Each call logged had either an "O" or an "I" next to it, and he guessed this identified them as outgoing or incoming. A

few names he knew from his background research on
Mtizito, a couple were dignitaries well-known in the galaxy. But as he was viewing the list marked "PC" upon
which were only a handful of names, he noticed a number
that seemed familiar, next to someone named "Thactor."

Cinch punched the number into his com's address book
and asked for a match.

Well, well. The com number was identical to that of
Sedih Peran's, supposedly an IAL for the Stellar Rangers.

Just for the hell of it, he tapped the other numbers on
that code into his com. None of them matched.

Thactor. Could Peran be using a pseudonym? That
wasn't impossible, though not likely. Why would he? And,
Cinch supposed, it would be normal for a legitimate IAL
to call on the local authorities—Peran had indicated that
he'd spoken with the governor. But all of the calls were
marked with an "I." If that meant all the calls were incoming, then he was lying about that, at least.

Thactor. As it happened, Cinch had the reader's triangu-
lar cursor on the name while he stared at it. He was
tapping idly at the reader's input board when he accidentally hit the spacebar. The name split.

Th Δ actor.

The actor . . . ?

Well. It could be a trick of the letters, he supposed, but
Cinch didn't believe that for a second. Lavan had hired an
actor to play an IAL. He knew something was wrong with
Peran but he'd assumed that maybe he'd been bribed. This
was better, because a legit inspector hadn't been bought; it
proved, at least to Cinch, that Lavan really was up to no
good.

It wasn't proof, of course. It was circumstantial and not
likely to convince a comp-judge or a human jury of much;
still, it was another bit he could add to the pile.

Cinch went through the other files. Most of them were
along the same lines insofar as hard evidence went. A lot
of arrows pointing toward Lavan's wrongdoing but not

enough to prove it. Zarant's spy had done pretty well, given that Lavan must be fairly circumspect. Maybe he would come up with more stuff yet.

Meanwhile, he'd better go and call Zarant and tell him about Chayne.

"Show me the layout," Lavan said. He was seated in his house, relaxing on the silk cushions of his couch, using his full-wall holoproj. The full-size image of Vita seemed to be standing only a few meters away.

"Okay," Vita's image said. He turned and started to walk.

The image shifted slightly as the camera operator's steadilens adjusted for his motion.

The expensive pistol he'd given Vita was strapped over his right hip, the leather fresh and unscratched. Lavan smiled.

"This is the reception room. There's normally three cools here, a desk officer, duty supervisor, and a com officer."

Lavan looked at the three imposters occupying those positions. They looked like real police officers, the uniforms genuine and the haircuts fresh. Surely they were enough to fool somebody moving past them in a hurry.

"Down this hall—this door is normally shut and locked—is the communal holding area. The individual cells are just past that. We moved all the prisoners out and replaced them with our people."

The communal cell held six men who looked more like thieves and substance abusers than the three out front Their final acting jobs, although they didn't yet know it.

"We got a woman in the cell next to O'thea's, in case she feels like talking."

"Don't bank on that," Lavan said.

"You never know."

The image shifted as the POV cam followed Vita to the end of the narrow corridor between the two rows of steel-barred cells, cages, really, most of which were empty. Inside the second to last one on the left, a blowsy woman of thirty lay on a pallet, smoking a cigarillo. Lavan spared her a moment of his attention. She was coarse enough to be trustworthy, if he followed Vita's logic.

Next to this woman in the final cell was Chayne O'thea. She was dressed in a white coverall and had a plastiskin bandage high on her left temple. She stood near the back wall, staring out as Vita arrived.

"Hello, bitch. Enjoying your stay?"

"Until just now."

Vita laughed. "Well. You won't be here long; we'll be hauling your sorry ass into the city for your trial and quick execution day after tomorrow."

O'thea didn't reply to this.

Lavan watched her. She couldn't see him, of course, any more than Vita could. She wasn't an ugly woman, quite attractive really, and from his brief contacts with her years earlier, very bright. But she'd picked the wrong issue to back and now she would pay for it. Too bad. He hated to waste good people more or less on principle, if it didn't get in the way of anything important. He could drop all of Vita's thugs into a vat of acid without a qualm, Vita, too, but O'thea and her paramour—he loved that quaint term— were idealists. They truly believed in what they were doing. In a perfect world, he would allow them to do such things, as long as it didn't interfere with business, of course. Lavan was not an unfeeling man. In fact, he liked to think of himself as fairly dedicated. After all, he had given years of service to the people of this planet with little thought for his own gain, until recently. Yes, he had been paid a salary for it, but in the beginning, he would have done it for free. And the salary was hardly anything, a pittance, really. He had picked up a little along the way, perks of the job, but the truth of it was, he had worked damned hard for the citizenry when you totaled it all up. And he'd been a damned good governor, all things considered. The streets were fairly safe, the mail got delivered, the buses ran on time. There were worse worlds.

"You just going to stand there and stare?" O'thea said. "You and that fat, murdering pig you work for?" She gestured palm up at the camera.

Lavan jerked on the couch, startled for an instant before he remembered she couldn't see him, she was only guessing. He supposed he couldn't blame her for taking it personally. After all, she was going to die.

"That's enough," Lavan said. Since Vita wore a button mike in one ear, he could hear that plainly. O'thea would not hear it at all.

"We'll see how smart you are when they pump the juice into you, cutthroat," Vita said. He turned and sidled past the camera. Lavan got a close-up of Vita's red beard as he almost brushed the steadilens. It looked like a forest of twisted and bent cables.

Back in the reception area of the police station, Vita looked directly into the camera again. "We got the place, uh ... *prepared* like you wanted. A different crew than anybody in here now. They, uh, that crew is taking a leave right now."

Lavan shook his head, ground his teeth, and wanted to strangle the man. If the mercenaries in here knew the place was wired to blow the damned building halfway to a weathersat's orbit, they'd be gone. Vita's idea of clever wordplay was pathetic. But Lavan forced himself to smile, even though Vita couldn't see him, and say, "Good. I'm sure you've handled things perfectly, Munga. I've dropped the information into a dozen channels. I'm sure the cutthroats will know about it soon enough."

"What if he doesn't come?"

"He will. We'll delay the 'move' an extra day if we have to, but don't worry. This guy thinks he's a hero. He won't let us just take his paramour and execute her."

"Para-what?"

Lavan shook his head again. The man was truly ignorant aside from being a fool.

"Never mind. Go and get out of sight. The clock is running."

After the connection was broken, Lavan went to fix himself a drink. As the glass chilled the champagne, he considered his options. This plan should work. Of course, he always thought that by the time he got this deeply into a plan, and even so, he had to keep his backup systems on full alert. If for some reason—and he couldn't really imagine one—Zarant did not come to fetch his companion, then at the very least there would be one less of them around. And Vita's endless whining would be stilled at the same time, so no matter what, things would not be a total loss.

He sipped the bubbly wine, savored the crisp yeasty taste of it. He'd have to figure out another way to get Zarant if this didn't work out and he supposed he should start looking around for other avenues to that end. But not just at this moment. He could allow himself the luxury of a glass of champagne now and then. Things couldn't get any worse during the course of a drink.

chapter 21

"I think we need to meet," Cinch said to Zarant.

"All right. Remember where you first saw Chayne? Go there."

Cinch ended the com and headed back toward his ATV. It was just after 1600, he had finished his dinner and used the public com in the bar next door to the restaurant. He grinned at that. If he had been following himself and had wanted to catch a possible call, he would have waited until he began eating, then had the whizzers tap the com in the restaurant's fresher, maybe even the one listed for the restaurant public calls to be sure. But there was no way to run around and get all the coms on the block coded and locked in during a short dinner and he wouldn't have even tried.

If they were surveilling him, they must be real frustrated.

It was a summer night and still daylight; should be light for another hour if a thunderstorm didn't build and thicken the evening. He hoped his ruse with Peran had them fooled. His cart hadn't been rebugged as far as he could tell, and if any tails were attached to him, he couldn't spot them.

Even if somebody did follow him to the burned-out

town where he'd first seen Chayne, he didn't think it likely they would find much there. Zarant wasn't stupid enough to be waiting for him.

The drive to Koma was relatively uneventful. Once he left the city and darkness finally dropped its curtain over him, the main problem he had was keeping the windscreen of the ATV clean. He must have used a liter of the cart's cleansing spray with the wipers to wash the smashed insects off the clear plastic; even so, the screen was smeared with bug bodies. One of them, a moth as big as his hands, left part of a powdery wing printed on the plastic as if it had been painted there, despite the cleaner and wiper. It looked like a large eye staring at him.

Lavan glanced into his chest of sexual toys, grinning. He'd had a taste of Murie and she'd worn him out, but that was yesterday. Tonight he was recharged. She had not been averse to the suggestion that she drop by his house and visit.

"I'll send a conveyance," he'd said.

"I'll be ready," she'd said.

Now, with all of the things he could do—all of the things he would eventually do, surely—it was too much to decide. He pushed the toys away. Let her decide. It was what he was going to be paying her for, wasn't it? She would hold back something, of course she would, she didn't want to give him all her secrets too soon, now did she? But she would offer up something special, too, to keep him interested.

He grinned wider. His sense of anticipation was piqued.

It couldn't get much better than this.

Cinch found a single-passenger air scooter parked next to the building where he'd first seen Chayne. It had been a tricky walk in the dark even with the spookeyes he wore. Clouds had rolled in to blanket the sky and there was no moon or starlight to speak of. The eyes couldn't amplify what wasn't there, and ambient nightglow was dim.

Stuck to the scooter's seat was a handwritten paper note.

"Take a ride," it said. "Call when you're twenty klicks away from here."

Cinch straddled the seat, lit the repellors, and slowly rose straight up. Once he cleared the buildings and trees he cycled the fans on and cruised away from the ruined town. He kept the scooter's lamps dark and zigzagged in sharp turns. He would bet his pistol nobody was following him.

Fifteen minutes later he commed Zarant.

"It's me. I'm on the scooter and in the middle of nowhere."

"Good. Open your modem and after the navicomp downloads the program, put the scooter on autopilot."

"Copy."

He followed Zarant's instructions.

Under the autopilot, the scooter made a long and wide turn, dropped to within seventy meters of the ground, and sped up considerably. The lights were still off.

Cinch hoped there weren't any really tall trees in his path.

Forty-five minutes later, after a course that changed enough to confuse him totally, the scooter's automatic controls shut down. The little craft dropped a couple of meters before Cinch took over. It was dark, but it was less cloudy and he still wore his spookeyes. He saw a tiny break in the trees to his left. He guessed he was where he was supposed to be.

He put the scooter down and shut the engines off. The repellor *ticked* as the circulating fluid cooled the hot metal. The burned fuel smell mixed with the damp tropical odor of the jungle at night, and the sounds of insects *chee-chee-cheed* around him. The cloud cover eased a little more and he was able to see better, everything washed in pale, spookeye green.

"C(!)arston," said a voice from behind him.

Cinch turned slowly. One of the *majivu* stood there, a gray-green ghost. He held his blowgun propped on the ground next to him like it was a spear.

"K(!)ree," Cinch said. "How's it going?"

"Pleezed to seeya, C(!)arston. Come on."

The gray man turned and started to pad away. Cinch followed him. As he did so, he saw three more of the *majivu* at the edge of the clearing, all armed with blowguns. He was pretty sure that if somebody else had climbed off the scooter, that person would be full of lizard venom right now. And if he hadn't spotted them with his augmented vision, it wasn't real likely anybody else would have seen them in time.

The gray men already knew about honor, he was pretty sure. Now, they were learning about guns. It was sad.

It was twenty minutes before they reached the campsite where Zarant waited for him. The two men clasped forearms and greeted each other.

Without preamble other than that, Cinch said, "I know where Chayne is."

Zarant nodded. Dim gas-mantle lamps cast a yellow glow over him. "Yeah. So do I."

Cinch said, "Hmm. How did you find out?"

"An old friend of mine from college heard it from somebody he knows in the state police. They're hiding her in a small station until they move her into the city for a trial."

Cinch nodded. "That's what I heard, too. Odd, though."

"Odd?"

"If they are hiding her, why is it that you and I both learned about it so fast? If they really wanted to keep it secret, we should have had to dig a little harder to uncover it. I didn't even have to ask—somebody called and gave it to me."

"You're saying they want us to know."

"It crossed my mind."

Zarant sighed. "Crossed mine, too. They know Chayne and I aren't just working together."

"If I were Lavan and I wanted you both out of the way—"

"—you'd use Chayne as bait for a trap."

"Yeah. I would."

Zarant rolled his head, stretching his muscles. He rubbed at the back of his neck. "What I figured. But I can't let them take her into the city and execute her."

"No, I don't see that you can."

"So, I have to figure a way around the trap."

"You know anything about the place where they're keeping her?"

Zarant grinned. "I know more about it than the people who built it. I've got the jail's construction plans, a map of the village, and four of the *majivu* with a com watching the place from the bush right now."

It was Cinch's turn to grin. "Good. Maybe you could show me what you've got?"

"In the tent."

Lavan slept the sleep of the dead. Had the building blown up, he probably wouldn't have awakened. He did dream, though, and the dream was full of Murie Vendle's hot and naked body in a palace packed with money. It was a great dream. Almost as great as the reality.

Zarant's intelligence was pretty good—he had holos, 2-D flats, and even transcribed reports from the *majivu*. He didn't have the exact cell in which Chayne was being held, but if he could get control of the police station and its tiny jail, a man in a hurry could find her in a minute or so, could the plans be believed.

"What do you think?" Zarant asked.

"Well. I'm a ranger and not a special services military op, but I've done a few hostage rescues. The principle is the same, I expect. Go in, bring 'em back alive."

"How would you rig a trap?"

Cinch looked at the plans, the aerial views of the station and surrounding town, the jungle where it crept to the edges of the local civilization.

"Offhand I can see a few ways. First, I'd make sure Chayne was really inside. If you found out somehow she wasn't, you wouldn't show up. I'd try to make things look as normal as possible from the outside, usual crew on duty, like that. Hide a whole lot of heavily armed troops, let you get inside, then surround the building. You might try to shoot your way out, but I'd have expert snipers set up and waiting. Try to run and we'd take you out. Try to stay inside, you wouldn't be able to hold off a siege for any kind of time, no food, no water."

Zarant nodded. "Yeah. But I'd have hostages of my own, cools, other prisoners."

"If Lavan is as bad as you say, I'd guess they'd be expendable."

"He is and you're probably right."

"Or he could try to take you in the woods on your way in."

"I thought about that. No matter how good they were at hiding, the *majivu* would spot them in the forest. They'd have to be stashed indoors, on a high circling aircraft, something."

"They probably know that."

Zarant sighed and looked at the holograph of the building from the air. "I don't think Lavan is particularly interested in taking us alive for a show trial. If we're gone and the *majivu* are scattered, he gets what he wants. If Chayne is in there"—he tapped the holograph with one finger— "and I go in, he can have his thugs open up on us with heavy artillery. Knock the building down on top of us."

"Another possibility."

Zarant stood inside the tent, his head nearly touching the low ceiling. He clenched his fists. Muscles danced and reshaped his forearms. "I have to get her out."

Cinch thought about how he would feel in Zarant's place. His connection with Chayne wasn't all that thick, a few hours together alone, and *he* was agitated enough to want to break her out. Zarant must be about to explode. Maybe it had all been philosophical before but it was surely personal now. If somebody had Cinch's wife and was threatening her life, he would do whatever it took to get her loose. And the people who had made the threat would be sorry they were ever born.

"You need a free pass."

"Excuse me?"

"A reason that Lavan's troops would hold off shooting."

"What do you mean?"

"Who is likely to be setting up the ambush?"

"Munga Vita."

"If you showed up with a hostage ... ?"

"Vita would laser his own mother if he thought it would gain him a bent tenth. The man has no morals about this kind of stuff; he would laugh as he pulled the trigger."

"Is there anybody he wouldn't shoot?"

"Only person I can think of might be our illustrious governor."

"There you go."

Zarant laughed. "You want to kidnap the *governor?*"

"You didn't hear that from me. My supervisors at SR HQ would probably frown on such a suggestion. But unofficially you might want to consider it. I would if I were you."

Zarant nodded. "Son of a bitch, that might work."

"After we get Chayne out, you can turn him loose."

" 'We?' "

"Like I said, officially I can't get involved in kidnapping. Unofficially, I might take a few days off from work. This is a nice little planet you got here. I could do some sightseeing."

Zarant laughed again. "I take it the rangers sometimes play a little loose with the regs."

"Now and again we have to look for the intent rather than the letter. Justice and the law are sometimes distant cousins. Seeing justice done is one of the things they pay us for."

"And if you screw up?"

Cinch shrugged. "I've been thinking about retiring."

"Okay. Why don't you take a few days off, Cinch? Let me show you around our nice little planet."

The two men smiled.

# chapter 22

When Cinch and Zarant emerged from the tent, Cinch felt the tension from the *majivu* as a tangible thing, almost as if they had spoken to him aloud.

"What's wrong?" he asked.

Zarant looked at him. "Wrong?"

"The *majivu* are upset. Is it just what has already happened, or something else?"

Zarant said, "Chayne was right, you are very perceptive. It's the storm."

Cinch almost asked "What storm?" before he remembered. "The hurricane?"

"Yes."

"Last weather report I heard, it had turned around and was heading in the other direction."

"May be, but the *majivu* say it's going to hit here within a few days."

Cinch didn't say anything but Zarant must have seen the skepticism on his face. The bigger man said, "The gray men have lived in the jungle for hundreds of thousands of years. They are in tune with the planet in a way civilized humans can never be. We've got climatesats, gigabyte computers, and people who have doctorates in both expounding on the weather, but when it gets right down to it,

163

if the *majivu* say it's going to rain and the forecasters say it won't, I'll bet on the *majivu* every time."

Cinch nodded. "Okay."

"We'd better get moving, a big storm might give us some problems."

Cinch flashed back to the hurricane with his grandfather all those years ago. "Or it might work to our advantage," he said.

Lavan stood in front of his window, staring out at the street below. The man behind him finished his report.

"So you think the *wembemvua* is going to turn?"

"We can't be sure, of course, but that unexpected high-pressure cell moving up from the southwest could cause that, yes. The storm could bounce right off it like a handball. Such things have been known to happen."

Outside, the tropical sunshine was bright enough to turn the polarized plastic window a dark gray. Hard-edged shadows painted the plastcrete as if they had been stenciled there. There was not a cloud in the sky.

"Well. Keep me informed."

The adviser left. One more brick on his load. God, he would be glad to get shut of this fucking job. It had all seemed so wonderful when he'd first been elected, but after all the years, the little day-to-day shit he had to endure was what made it so bad. It was one thing to win the job, another thing entirely to have to *do* it.

From the outer office, Pakita said, "The Youth Scouts have arrived."

Christ on a stretcher. Another holograph session with a bunch of children. It was a wonder the human race didn't die out, given that children were the main penalty you sometimes had to pay for sex. How could anyone stand to be around the little brats all the time? Twenty minutes in front of a camera with a horde of the small demons and he was ready to have them all thrown into the nearest body of deep water. Amazing that people put up with them.

"Fine." He put on his professional smile and started for the door.

Cinch, Zarant, and five of his men sat in the back of a hovertruck disguised with furniture-moving logos as it cruised down one of the city's main streets. It was 0945 and the promise of a blazing afternoon was already manifesting itself. Fortunately the inside of the van was cooled. Otherwise, they would be cooking under the bare metal ceiling, too hot to touch even now.

"He's going to lunch at noon," Zarant said. "Afterward, he has an assignation with a corporate VP from IGM. She is his latest sexual partner; they'll meet at his house and be there for at least three hours."

"How do you know?"

"His schedule is blocked out until 1500. According to our spy."

Cinch said, "Security?"

"Hardly any. Our governor thinks of himself as a benevolent and well-liked man. He has a couple of capitol police officers who attend public functions with him dressed as civilians, and an alarm system at his house, but normally he doesn't travel with bodyguards. Not good for his image."

Cinch shook his head. If he were the governor and had Zarant and his irregulars running around in the jungle only a few hundred klicks away, he would certainly have at least a few cools watching his ass. True, a really determined assassin could get to almost anybody, providing the assassin was willing to die in the process, but a well-trained bodyguard could stop less fanatic types. Either the governor wasn't very bright about such things, or he was supremely arrogant and thought himself untouchable.

"So what is your plan?"

"We have the repair access codes to his alarm system," Zarant said. "When he gets there, we'll be waiting."

It seemed too simple to Cinch, but sometimes the most effective plans happened to work out that way.

"You sure you don't want to come along?"

"Better not."

"Well. I'll wear a hatcam. You can watch from here."

Lavan arrived at his house with Murie. They alighted from the limo and he waved it away. The driver would return at 1500; until then, he didn't want anybody around save the two of them. Down the road a bit a furniture truck sat parked in front of Thruse's house. Lavan shook his head. The old man must be buying another piano, he had nine of the damned things in his place, bad enough, but he was also as tone-deaf as a lamppost.

Murie held on to his arm with both hands as they walked to the front entrance. She'd skipped dessert at the restaurant, she'd said, because she planned to eat something else later. A much better way to spend her time and his calories.

He grinned. The woman was like a fine wine or a drug. He could easily get used to having her around all the time. True, that might blunt his appetites somewhat, having her available whenever he wished, but that would not happen for a while.

He put his right hand on the security reader and the front door slid silently open. She dropped her left hand to his groin as they stepped inside, as if she couldn't wait to touch him. Very good at this, she was.

After the door shut behind them and she found he was ready for any activities requiring tumescence, a deep male voice said, "Good afternoon to you, Governor. And Fem Vendle."

Lavan jerked, startled, and turned to see a man sitting on his couch. Well, not so much sitting as sprawled. He was a big, tanned man with long black hair tucked under a short-brimmed cap, wearing a tropical-weight polyprop khaki shirt and shorts. Even relaxed, the man's musculature was impressive, ridges and swellings in his arms and legs denoting great physical power.

Zarant. Here, in his house!

Lavan's mind twirled, a tornado of confused thoughts. What was he doing here? Assassination? Did he want to make some kind of deal? If he had a weapon, it wasn't apparent. He was smarter than Lavan had figured. He hadn't gone for the bait; he must know it was a trap. He had bypassed the obvious and now he was *here*. That was it— the man had come to bargain for his captured companion. Yes, that had to be it. He was here to offer some kind of a trade. Lavan could lead him along, agree to whatever he wanted, and then spike him at the first chance. Yes. That was how he would play it.

"You've come about O'thea," Lavan said. He strived to seem offhand, unconcerned, in control.

"Yes."

To Vendle, he said, "Murie, this is Laird Zarant, one of the little details I mentioned to you that remained to be cleared up before we could proceed with our . . . arrangement?"

Taking Lavan's lead, Murie smiled at Zarant.

"Well, then," Lavan said. "Let me fix you a drink and we'll discuss the matter."

"Oh, I don't think we have enough time for that," Zarant said. "It's a long ride to Pos Restant. We want to get there while there is plenty of daylight left so nobody makes any mistakes."

Lavan blinked. "What?"

"We're all going for a little ride, a nice jaunt in the country."

Lavan wasn't a paranoid man, but he did know that there were always people who focused their irritation with government upon those who led it. His guards were for show, mostly, to keep the crowds from pressing too close, but he did have the means to protect himself in his own house, if need be. A drunk had once pounded on his door in the middle of the night, seeking satisfaction for some real or imaginary grievance, and from that point on, Lavan had kept several weapons around, out of sight but located where he could get to them easily.

He had one of those guns crowed to the underside of the bar.

To Zarant he said, "Well, maybe you don't want a drink but if I'm going back out into the heat, I need one." He moved smoothly toward the bar.

Zarant remained sprawled on the couch, turning only his head to watch Lavan as he moved toward the bar.

Better make it look good, Lavan thought. He opened the cooler, removed a bottle of mineral water, set it on the bar directly over where he knew the gun was attached. He took a chiller from a shelf, triggered it, and watched the frost form on the glass as he set it onto the counter. He pretended to be waiting for the chiller to finish its cold cycle, smiling broadly at Zarant as he carefully and casually slipped one hand under the bar . . .

"Sorry, Yogen, but it's not there," a woman's voice said.

Startled again, Lavan looked toward the doorway into his kitchen and saw Pakita standing there, holding a pistol.

"Pakita! Thank God! Quick, shoot him!" He pointed at Zarant.

It was only when she and Zarant smiled that it occurred to him to wonder what his secretary was doing here. And he wasn't slow coming up with the answer.

"You bitch," Lavan said. He was so angry his voice quavered.

Betrayed!

"Now, now, Yogen," she said. "We need you alive but I could put a needle through your leg, say, and you would be in a lot of pain. Or I could aim a little higher and maybe damage something you value a lot more than your leg." She waved the gun, then looked at Murie and smiled at her. "Though it's a pretty small target this far away, eh, sister?"

Pakita held up her free hand and spaced her thumb and forefinger a couple of centimeters apart.

Lavan wanted to scream. He would kill her. He would have them all thrown into a kennel of hungry dogs!

Zarant stood, a fluid motion. "Let's go."

From inside the disguised truck, Cinch watched, courtesy of the hatcam Zarant wore. He smiled. Pakita, the woman he'd met at the governor's office, the woman he'd assumed was there for things other than simple secretarial duties, was Zarant's spy. Well, he'd been right about her being something other than what she'd appeared to be, even though he'd been wrong about exactly what.

Well. So far, so good. They had Lavan, nobody had jumped out of a closet blasting, the street outside the house was quiet and, as far as Cinch could tell, they weren't being watched.

So far, so good.

chapter 23

"You won't get away with this, you know," Lavan said. He saw the furniture van parked down the street start, lift in a cloud of grit, and fan slowly toward where they stood. Pakita still had the gun—his gun, the one from under the bar, dammit—only now it was hidden under a fold of her silks.

Murie said to Zarant, "You'll want to contact my company to discuss my ransom. Or perhaps we can work something out, you and I."

The slut!

"I don't think that will be necessary, Fem Vendle. After we finish our business, you'll be released. Assuming that the governor's people don't do anything stupid, nobody'll get hurt."

"Listen, Zarant," Lavan said as the frontwash of the van blew a wave of dust at them, "you don't know what you're doing. It isn't just Mtizitonian authorities you're dealing with anymore. You're stepping on galactic toes. The rangers are here—you know that, you met the guy."

"So I did."

The van idled past, floating on its GE cushion. The rear door rolled up with a clatter. "Inside," Zarant said. "And if you think about running, Pakita will shoot you. She's an expert with a handgun, by the way. She can hit a hand-sized target at twenty meters all day long."

Lavan had already considered trying to run but rejected the idea. He had been, in his younger days, a man willing to take chances with his life. He'd hunted big cats on the Tukwila Reserve, worked briefly on the floating petroleum rigs as a hardhand on vacations from the university, had punched tough men and women out in bar brawls. For a time he'd been in the political action group Sabtu Malam—nobody had ever accused them of being afraid to bust heads, and he'd caved in a few skulls during that period. But those days were long past, and his plan of living for a thousand years would hardly come to pass if he got shot by a bunch of five-and-demicee *environmentalists* on the fucking street in front of his own house. Zarant could break him in half with one hand and he had no doubt that Pakita would put a needle in him where it would hurt the most. After the stuff he'd made her do—hell, he thought she'd liked some of it, at least—he could see she might not feel too kindly toward him. And no matter her expertise, a badly placed shot could accidentally kill him.

No, he was outmatched in brawn. He'd have to outwit them.

"Think about it. You don't want the rangers mad at you, Zarant."

Zarant smiled. "No, I sure don't, do I, Cinch?"

"Not generally a good idea," someone said from inside the truck.

Lavan stared, unable to believe what he was seeing.

Carston! The fucking ranger!

As the hovertruck fanned along the streets at a stately, legal pace, the ten people on the benches inside sat quietly, not speaking.

Cinch had to admit, if only to himself, that he'd much enjoyed the expression on the governor's face when the man saw him waiting inside. "This is outrageous! You can't be allied with this—this thug! You're a *ranger!* And I'm the governor of this planet!"

"Yes, sir, you're right. Thing is, the rangers are concerned with truth more than we are rank or social status. I've seen enough to convince me that you're dirtier than the windows on a wartime crematorium."

"You can't prove anything!"

"I expect I can prove some of it. Maybe not all of what I believe, but enough to keep you from killing the *majivu* off and selling their land to Fem Vendle's employers."

The VP glanced at Lavan, then back at Cinch. "Please understand, ranger, that my corporation has no knowledge of any illegal activities regarding this matter and under no circumstances would we knowingly be party to felonious acts." It was a set speech, probably one she'd given on more than a few occasions, and Cinch merely nodded.

Lavan turned to stare at the woman. "Christ, you cunts are all alike, aren't you? Listen, when this is done, you can forget about any personal arrangement we might have had. You just stabbed *yourself* in the back, bitch."

Vendle smiled at him, almost sweetly, then turned to where Pakita sat across from her. "You were right," she said. She held her hand up, thumb and forefinger a couple of centimeters apart.

The governor flushed under his white beard.

Cinch smiled.

The ride took a couple of hours and ended ten klicks short of the town of Pos Restant. Zarant's men stayed with the truck while Pakita took the IGM VP away in a smaller vehicle. Cinch, Zarant, and Lavan entered a third cart, a somewhat beat-up runabout with its convertible top up. Cinch drove, Lavan sat in the back with Zarant, who was now armed with a big pistol he held pressed into the governor's side.

"Anything happens to surprise or annoy me, I empty

this thing into you," Zarant said, nudging Lavan with the weapon.

Lavan's already pale skin ghosted a little whiter.

"Here's how it's going to go," Zarant continued. "A little way from here, Cinch is going to stop the car and get out. Then you get to drive and the two of us are going to pull right up to the front door of the police station. You and I will get out and go inside. By the way, did I mention this pistol has a deadman's trigger set to full auto? See, as long as I am holding it still, nothing happens. But if something makes me let go of it, like, oh, I don't know, a hidden sniper shoots a high-velocity round through my head, then the gun goes off and puts all fifteen of its explosive bullets into you in something like a half second. Sounds a lot like somebody tearing a sheet of canvas on full auto, *rrrriiip!* Maybe the best medics in the galaxy could put you back together, assuming they could find enough of the mush that used to be your heart and lungs and liver to even try."

Lavan sweated despite the cart's air cooler.

"Inside, we fetch Chayne and then leave. If anybody screws with the cart while we're gone, whatever happens to it will happen to you. I have people watching the door, some of whom have very sharp eyes."

Cinch said nothing but he didn't need to. Zarant was playing his part perfectly.

"After we get far enough away, and assuming nobody follows us, we let you go."

"I'm supposed to believe that?"

"Believe what you like. That's the deal. I might be tempted to shoot you on general principles, but the ranger here won't go along with that. He thinks he's got enough for the law to take care of you and he wants to see you explaining things to a judge."

"My people won't know about the deadman's trigger on your gun," Lavan said. His voice was a hoarse croak. He wasn't going to pretend the station was anything but a trap. "They might shoot you."

"Then maybe you'd better fill them in on the revised plan." He pulled a com from his pocket and handed it to the governor.

Lavan took the com and tapped in a number manually. "It's me."

The voice that responded said, "Yeah? Everything is set, but no sign of him yet."

Lavan glanced at Zarant, who smiled politely.

"There's been, uh, a slight change in the situation."

"What?"

"I'm sitting in the back of a cart with Zarant right now and he's got a gun with a deadman's trigger stuck in my ribs."

"Shit. You're kidding, right?"

"No, I'm *not* kidding. He's outmaneuvered us on this one. He and I are going to go into the station, get O'thea, and then leave. Don't do anything to get in our way, do you understand?"

"Jesus, Yogen—"

"Nothing! We go in, we come out, nobody does *shit!* You understand that? If Zarant trips, I'm a dead man. Tell your troops to back off and tell the men inside exactly how it is going to happen."

"I—yeah, yeah, I hear you. Nobody does anything."

"I'll get back to you later," Lavan said.

Zarant took the com back and pocketed it. "You did good, Governor."

Lavan licked his lips. "Listen, Vita isn't reliable. You heard me tell him to back off, but I don't trust him."

"No honor among thieves?"

"This isn't funny, Zarant. You could get us all killed."

Zarant glanced up at Cinch via the mirror on the dash, then back at Lavan. "There's something you aren't telling me, isn't there? What was your plan? Exactly how did you plan to spring the trap?"

Cinch watched the man's face in the mirror. He could almost see the gears whirling as the governor tried to come up with a story that would satisfy Zarant.

"My hands are all sweaty," Zarant said. "My finger could slip on this trigger any time."

"You need me!"

"Maybe not. Maybe Chayne is already dead."

"No, she's alive. I swear."

"Or maybe she's not there. Maybe we get inside an empty building and the roof falls in on us."

Lavan sucked in a quick breath.

*Touched a nerve,* Cinch thought.

Zarant caught it, too. "Damn. That's it, isn't it? You've got the building rigged to blow, don't you?"

Lavan rubbed at his mouth, not speaking. He didn't need to.

Zarant moved the pistol up to touch Lavan's temple. "You know, maybe a great surgeon could do a massive organ transplant even if all your guts were shot out. Maybe they could keep you alive on machines without a heart or lungs. But if I blew your brains all over the inside of this cart—"

"Yes! Yes, goddammit, the building is wired! Enough to turn everybody in it into bloody goo!"

Cinch said, "Not likely to happen with the governor inside, though, is it?"

"There's got to be another way," Lavan said hastily. "We don't need to go in; I can call, order them to send her out!"

"You really don't trust Vita, do you?"

"He's greedy and he's stupid," Lavan said. "If he thought killing me along with you and O'thea would gain him anything, he would do it in a second. He can't pull the deal off on his own but I'm sure he thinks he can. He would kill ten thousand people, grinning all the while, for the money involved here!"

Cinch wished he had thought to trigger his recorder.

This was great conspiracy stuff. The rules of evidence wouldn't allow this gunpoint kind of confession, of course. Too bad, even though he understood the principle.

To Zarant, Cinch said, "Maybe we ought to revise the revised plan a hair."

"What did you have in mind?"

Cinch watched the cart with Zarant and Lavan pull away. He moved off the street between two buildings where a three-wheeled ground scooter had been left for him. He found the keycard under the floormat, started the electric motor and rolled from the alley toward the rendezvous point. If Lavan were right about Vita, there was still some risk, but maybe they could still pull it off. No guarantees, but then again, there never were in situations like this.

You had to work with what you had. And keep your expectations at bay.

Lavan felt a jagged boulder of ice form in his belly as they alighted from the cart in front of the police station. Vita probably wouldn't have them shot—the snipers might hesitate to do that when they could see a gun in his side. They couldn't be sure to get Zarant before he could kill his hostage. At least he hoped so.

But once inside . . .

Vita had the trigger and was primed to use it. His orders had been to kill O'thea and Zarant, but if the governor were inside, why, so much the better. Lavan was sure of it. With him out of the way, Vita would think of himself as the man in charge. He wasn't an intellectual giant on his best days and Lavan knew how he thought: It would all be so neat. Nobody in his way anymore.

He would push the fucking detonator, Lavan was certain of that, as sure as he was of anything. Only nothing he could say made any difference. Zarant was as crazy as Vita, more so. They were going to die, blown to bits, and there wasn't a damned thing he could do to stop it. It was no consolation at all that Vita would die at the same instant, destroyed by the explosive hidden in his fancy new pistol's grips.

Inside, the men masquerading as cools could not hide their surprise at seeing him, even though Vita had supposedly told them he was coming.

"Take us to the prisoner," Lavan said.

"But, uh . . ."

"Now, stupid. Don't you see the fucking gun in my side?"

"Y-Yessir."

The fake cool hurried to open the doors for them.

Lavan hated the look on O'thea's face when she saw them. The fucking smile that blossomed. He hated them, hated Vita, hated Murie Vendle. Hated everybody at that moment. This was all wrong! This wasn't how it was supposed to be. He didn't have a backup for this!

"Laird—"

"No time, Chayne. Hurry."

Her cell door opened, the woman hustled out. Zarant leaned over toward the nervous guard and said, "Give me your keycard."

The man quickly obeyed.

Zarant looked at the card, then at the guard. "Better go tell your pals that this place is rigged to blow up," the big man said. "Bombs in the walls, you understand? Somebody is going to drop this building, probably in the next few seconds. Get everybody out, fast."

"Shit!" the man said.

He turned and ran. Slipped and almost fell, but managed to keep to his feet as he cleared the door screaming:

"Bomb, there's a bomb!"

"All right, this way," Zarant ordered Lavan.

"What are you doing? That's not the way—"

"Back exit. Move!"

They ran.

It seemed as if it took a long time to reach the door. Like running in a dream. Only if they didn't get out quickly, they weren't going to wake up from this nightmare.

chapter 24

The jail opened onto an alley that wasn't particularly narrow but offered no hiding places at ground level other than an open trash bin slightly larger than a cart. There might be shooters on the buildings lining the alley, but unless somebody was in the bin, nobody could get very close to the door itself.

The timing on it was tricky. Cinch and Pakita sped into the alley in one of the larger carts, a four-seater with the main electrics protesting, and they slewed to a stop by the rear fire exit of the jail.

Pakita drove, Cinch rode shotgun, and he jumped out and flung the door wide, his pistol held in port-ready position as he spun and scanned the alley.

The door burst open. Lavan ran out first, followed closely by O'thea and Zarant.

"Go, go, go!" Pakita yelled.

It was a tight fit as the three piled into the cart's rear seat. As soon as they were in, Cinch shoved his pistol toward the trash bin and capped off two rounds. The double sonic *boom!* was loud in the confines of the alley, and the *clack-clack!* of the two lead starfish bullets smacking into the heavy plastic would probably sound louder still to anybody hiding inside. Somebody in there would sure as hell keep his or her head down, at least for a moment.

Cinch jumped into the cart's front seat and Pakita had it rolling before he could reach for the door to shut it. The motors complained again, whining and laboring, as the cart picked up speed.

Cinch happened to be looking up when the sniper peered over the roof of the building next to the jail, a scoped rifle in his hands. The sniper had a bad angle, shooting almost straight down, but if he or she was a pro—Cinch couldn't see the sniper's face for the helmet's visor—they could be in trouble. He thrust his pistol through the cart's open window and unloaded the remaining four rounds from the antique Smith at the man or woman on the roof. The angle wasn't any better from here and he saw one of the rounds splash against the synstone a good three meters shy of the sniper. But it was enough to make the sniper pull back.

They were less than a hundred meters away from the jail's back door when the station blew.

Lavan heard the bombs go off, a noise louder than anything he'd ever experienced, and he scrunched lower in the seat and covered his head with his arms. The cart rocked, tipped to his left enough for him to have a moment of panic that it would flip over onto its back. But it fell back onto all four wheels again with a jolt that rattled his clenched teeth. It also sounded as if they were rolling through a bad hailstorm as tiny bits of debris pattered against the cart's side and roof. The back windscreen cracked and starred.

"Fuck!" somebody yelled. He could not have said who, maybe it was him.

But they were alive and moving, and Lavan was clear enough to be outraged at Vita. The late Munga Vita, who certainly deserved death for what he'd just done.

"Hang on!" Pakita yelled, as the cart hit something solid

and battered through it, twisting the vehicle and putting it into a momentary sideways skid.

*"Fuck!"* somebody yelled again. This time Lavan was pretty sure it was Pakita who said it.

The cart left the alley in a sharp turn, nearly leaving the ground at the same time.

Somebody in a combat uniform, softsuit armor, and a carbine leaped out into the street in front of them. The ranger was reloading his weapon and while Zarant still had his pistol, he was in no position to shoot. The trooper raised the carbine.

Pakita hit him with the cart. The *thump!* was quite loud and very solid. The cart's left front panel shattered from the impact and left most of the shredded plastic shards behind with the unfortunate trooper.

Zarant punched out the damaged rear screen and pointed his pistol through it, but there were no signs of pursuit.

Lavan looked back and saw the street in front of what had been the police station. It was filled with dark smoke and dust, and there was a heap of rubble stretched out and piled against the buildings across the street. It was at least a meter high in the center of the road and mounded like a giant snowdrift to three times that where it lay against the other structures.

*Jesus.*

"I were you, I'd fire Vita," Zarant said as he turned back to look at Lavan.

"I already have."

Three klicks from the destroyed jail, Pakita pulled the damaged cart to a stop next to a similar vehicle. "Time to switch rides," she said.

There were a few passersby, on their way toward the roiling smoke that filled the sky, but none of them took notice of the five exiting the cart.

Cinch looked at Zarant as the big man alighted. Zarant nodded at him wordlessly. He turned to Lavan. "Okay,

Governor. We drive away and you'll have to find your own ride, I'm afraid."

"You're letting me go?"

"I said I would, didn't I? What's the matter, you not used to dealing with people who keep their word?"

The governor just shook his head, obviously amazed to be alive and about to be granted his freedom. If the situation were reversed, Cinch was pretty sure they'd all be history real fast.

"Let's go, Pakita."

As the four of them entered the car, Zarant turned to the still-amazed Lavan. "I expect we'll be seeing each other again," he said.

Lavan stared at him.

"Oh. One last little item—there's no such thing as a deadman's trigger, not on handguns, anyway."

Zarant grinned and waved as the cart pulled away.

Lavan stood there staring after them until they rounded the next curve.

Once again Cinch rode in the front passenger seat, with Zarant and O'thea in the back. At the moment they were hugging, clutching at each other like long-lost lovers. Cinch turned his attention back to the road in front of them, then to Pakita.

"So, you're the spy."

"It was a nasty job but somebody had to do it."

She drove the cart expertly. "Before I became 'Pakita,' the governor's private whore, I was Kérsin Dompét, one of Professor Zarant's graduate students."

Cinch raised an eyebrow.

"Sometimes the end does justify the means, ranger."

"I hear you."

For a time, they rode in silence. Pakita—Kérsin—drove along a circuitous route that wound quickly from the town onto a narrow road bounded by jungle. After a while, she turned along an even narrower track, hardly more than a bumpy path, and followed it for another klick or so. When she stopped the cart, the foliage came to within centimeters of the vehicle on the sides and completely hid it from any overhead view.

Cinch turned to look at Zarant and O'thea, who now sat rather sedately holding hands and grinning.

"Thanks, Cinch," Zarant said.

Chayne nodded. "Yeah, me, too."

Cinch felt a small twinge of something deep in his chest. He had slept with this woman, he liked her a lot, and he would bet that she cared for him, too. But they were a couple, Zarant and O'thea, and he couldn't expect to be more than icing on her cake. On the one hand he didn't begrudge them their primacy; on the other hand, he wondered what it would be like to have somebody willing to die for him. To have a true mate and a place in which to love her. He'd been a wanderer all his life—the rangers merely gave him an excuse to indulge it—and now, he found that it was no longer enough. He wanted a place and a person to be with him in that place, family, friends, roots.

Maybe it wouldn't be here. Maybe it would be on some other world, but he felt it to the center of his being: it was time to hang up his gun and badge, prop his feet up on a porch rail, and watch the children run in the yard.

Assuming he didn't get killed here first, of course. Now that the governor knew where Cinch stood, he was going to have to be a bit more ... circumspect. Even getting offworld was apt to be a bit sticky.

Well—

"Cinch?"

He refocused on here and now. Chayne looked at him. "Where'd you go?"

"I was just thinking about a woman named Wanita I know. I think you might like her."

"If you do, I'm sure I could probably come to like her." Cinch nodded.

Then a trio of gray men coalesced from the shadows and came to stand next to the cart. If these guys ever wanted to get jobs as jungle fighters, they'd have no trouble passing the camouflage test.

"Time to take a little walk," Zarant said.

"Where is Vita?" the governor asked one of the troopers searching the rubble of the police station for bodies. Other troopers kept dozens of onlookers back behind an orange plastic ribbon.

"I dunno, Governor. Nobody's seen him since the explosion."

*Damned right about that,* Lavan thought. Aloud he said, "Well, if you spot him, I'll be at the hotel across the way there."

"Uh, Governor, do you know what happened here?"

"There was an explosion."

"Uh, yeah, I know that, I mean, do you know why?"

"Something blew up."

Lavan turned away. What a fiasco. He had to do some serious thinking about all this. The deal with IGM was probably shot, given his last encounter with that slut who represented them. O'thea and Zarant were loose and heading a group of killer apes. Vita was soypro burger splattered all over a wall somewhere. The fucking ranger had some kind of evidence, or said he did, that would put the governor in a bad situation if he had to explain his actions to galactic authorities. And Pakita, lovely compliant Pakita of the talented mouth and hands and other moist places, was a goddamned spy who probably did have enough evidence to allow the ranger to bury him in dog shit up to his eyeballs.

No, this was not good. He had to take stock, and quickly, and decide how he was going to overcome these obstacles that had been thrust so maliciously into his path.

chapter 25

"I think I would have shot him," Chayne said to Zarant.

"In either of your places, I'd have been tempted to shoot him, too," Cinch added.

"We had a deal," Zarant said. "All I wanted was you. Cinch here'll take care of Lavan. Legally."

Cinch give them a wry smile. "I hope."

The three of them sat in a six-person tent, set up under a tree canopy so thick they had a lantern lit so they could see, even though it was two hours yet until dark. The camp was in a different place than before and the number of humans and gray men in it had been reduced. Only combatants were left—those too young or too old to fight were gone, taken deep into the forest and hidden. From here on out, Zarant said, things were going to be different. Vita and his men would venture into the bush at their peril.

"You think that's wise?" Cinch asked.

"No. But the *majivu* are tired of running and hiding, and so am I. If every time one of Lavan's people sticks his nose into the woods somebody shoots at it, maybe they'll think twice about it."

"You can't win a stand-up fight."

"Don't plan to. We'll do it the way Khadaji did on Greaves, or the Harimau did it against the Pure Stockers on Souafra. Guerrilla warfare, hit-and-run. Until the people on this planet realize that the *majivu* are sentient beings who were here first."

Cinch shook his head. "Or until the *majivu* are all dead."

"Same difference," Zarant said. "This way at least we make it cost them something."

"It'll be a lot easier if you get Lavan out of the way," Chayne said. "He is the main snag in the path. There are those in the city who will listen to reason if they aren't looking over their shoulders for a knife aimed at their backs."

"I'll do what I can," Cinch said.

"We know that," Chayne said. "But Laird is right. Meanwhile, we have to stand up for our own rights as best we can. The days of Manifest Destiny and the stronger-culture-always-wins ought to be gone."

A rumble in the distance sounded at first to Cinch like an aircraft, then he recognized it as thunder. "Sounds like a shower coming," he said.

"More than a shower," Zarant said. "The razor rains are on the way. Come on, we've got to get packed and move. We'll need more than tents to keep the weather off. We'll go to the Root Caves."

"Root Caves?"

"A place of refuge the *majivu* have. It's three hours from here, to the northeast. Even if the storm holds together long enough to reach there with any speed, we should be okay."

Cinch nodded. He had to think about his next move anyway. One place was as good as another to do that, but in a hurricane, some spots were definitely better than others.

Lavan watched the scud from the *wembemvua* as the oily off-white clouds flitted across a sky the color of zinc and old lead. Damned forecasters didn't know what the hell they were about most of the time and this was more proof of it. The storm was heading straight at the city, which was far enough inland so the winds would be slowed some by the time it got here; still, sustained winds near the center were clocking almost four hundred klicks an hour. Half that velocity would be bad enough for a city not used to such storms. Emergency Response was already rolling in top gear, evacuating low-lying areas and housing deemed too flimsy to survive hard winds. Local markets had mostly sold out of batteries, generators, and water purification units, and nobody could stock toilet wipes fast enough to keep them on the shelves. It was one of the few times canned food held a premium over fresh, too.

A fucking razor rain was not what Lavan needed right now. Just one more grain on his scale.

He hadn't gone home after the bombing in Pos Restant. Instead, he'd had himself driven to his recreation cabin twenty klicks southeast of the city, where he could be alone to think. The decision he had to make was major, as big as any he'd ever made before.

Should he cut his losses and run? Or stay and ride out the storm—and not just the tropical one blowing toward the mainland, but the legal one that might follow? *Would* follow.

He could try to find and take out the ranger, of course, but he was afraid things had gone too far for that. There was Pakita, who doubtless had records of things he would rather she didn't have. He had been careful most of the time, but he hadn't been concerned about her. She'd been like furniture, there, but forgotten save when he needed her services. Damn. It never occurred to him that Pakita was anything other than a simpleminded servant willing to exchange sexual favors for security and a certain amount of prestige. A stupid mistake on his part.

Pakita worked for Zarant, and if she had given him a machete, Lavan could be certain that Zarant would gleefully hack the governor to small pieces with it. If not the ranger or Zarant, then O'thea. Somebody who had reason to hate him would surely wind up with the information. That was bad.

True, he had influence, money, and a power base here. If trouble were to come from the local authorities, then it wouldn't be a real problem. But local strength didn't cook much plasma with galactic prosecutors. They loved to come into a backrocket world and stomp the crap out of wrongdoers. They carried large sticks, the galactic prosecutors did, and big dogs in a little yard were that much easier to see and hit with those large sticks.

Lavan had been in politics long enough to know that people you thought were your friends would vanish faster than a ship hitting Salinas warp if a bigger dog arrived and showed its teeth. Sure, he had millions stashed and he could fight a long time and real hard, hire the best legals, blow a lot of smoke, drag it out. It was easy to hide stuff when nobody was really looking for it. But he was guilty of a whole lot of things and, once they started digging, some of those things were going to come to light. Sooner or later, he would lose. They'd root around and find most of his money, slap him in rehab for years, fill him full of chem and platitudes and, in the end, that would be that. In his heart, he knew it. Galactic prosecutors were like *leeta* eels—once they bit, they never let go.

Which left the second option.

He could convert most of his wealth into hard curry and stones, pack a bag, and hit the starlanes. He had a dozen false IDs ready against the day when something like this might happen, and a rich man could move in ways a poor man could not. Leave before the heat arrived, find a nice comfortable world where he could blend in, and regroup. No, he wouldn't have the megamonies he would need for the longevity treatments; then again, he wouldn't be in rehab and broke, either, a better deal no matter how you looked at it. And with a few million, he could still be a player, albeit a smaller one than he wished. A man with a sharp mind and a pocket full of coin could figure something out. He could bootstrap himself upward. Maybe get to where he wanted to go by another route. At least there was a chance.

Lavan took a deep breath and let it out. Yes. It made more sense to move on. It was a big galaxy, they'd never find him if he were careful, and it actually felt liberating in one whole way. He'd be without baggage wherever he went, healthy, not too old, well-off enough so he could live high. Playing out a normal span as a moderately rich man was a hell of a lot better than spending the rest of his life or a good portion of it locked away in a galactic prison.

Okay. Run it is.

The decision made, the thing was best done quickly, too. Before the damned storm got here and threw another boulder into his path, he would zip things shut and get out.

He went to his computer and began the process of gathering his portable money. A few kilos of platinum coins, a couple of small bags of first water diamonds and emeralds small enough to sell without raising eyebrows, maybe seven or eight million in all. Plus there were some offworld securities he could eventually get to if he moved quickly enough. Not bad. Not great, but it could have been a lot worse. Now was not the time to be greedy. Given a week, he could put together twice as much, but he didn't have a week, or at least he didn't want to spend it. Eight million today was a lot better than no million tomorrow.

There was a ship at the North Base kept in readiness to lift at short notice and he gave that notice. No customs, no questions. He had a few minor chores to finish, a couple of personal items he couldn't leave behind, and that was pretty much it. The major artwork, the custom orthopedia, the handmade vehicles, and other toys would have to stay behind. Too bad, but not really that expensive a price to pay for freedom.

In a few hours he would be ready.

Outside, the wind was picking up.

* * *

The carts bumped along the rugged trails, the motion lulling Cinch into a half doze broken now and then by a jolt when they hit a rock or a snag larger than the others. The screened windows were open and a fresh breeze that was cool as evening arrived. There didn't seem to be as many insects smacking into the screens as usual.

"Even the bugs know it's coming," Zarant said.

Cinch nodded. The air did have that prestorm damp smell, and even somebody with his blunted connection to the land could feel the impending sense of something unusual about to happen.

"Coming up on the place soon," Chayne said.

Cinch allowed the rocking motion of the cart to keep him in twilight sleep for however long it took. It was fully dark when the carts stopped, but a storm pod whose lightning flashes outreached its rain lit the scene enough for him to see the place they'd called the Root Caves. And it was pretty impressive.

*"Djaris do T(!)uhan,"* K(!)ree said.

"The Fingers of God," Chayne translated.

Cinch could see why they called it that. An interconnecting series of boabablike trees—or maybe it was a single tree—extended up into the windy night. The trees weren't particularly tall, but they were huge at the bases, and the root system began three or four meters above the ground and spread outward like stiff tentacles, or the fingers of a multitude of giant hands. The roots were not straight, but woven back and forth into a kind of thick and twisty mesh whose thinner sections were as big around as a man's arm. Some of the humps had been lined with something that matched the color, what he could see of it, to form enclosures. It looked to Cinch like nothing so much as a series of crude domes with trees growing out of the rooftops.

"Three hundred or so years ago, near as we can figure, the Bawang River jumped its banks and cut its way through here. Must have been a real rainy season, the Bawang now runs almost thirty klicks east of here. The loop it sent this way dried up pretty quick; it didn't kill the trees, just dug the dirt away and left the roots exposed. You can see the knees the roots put out—it had to have been about five meters deep here long enough for that to happen."

Another distant flash of lightning strobed the grove.

Zarant continued. "The *majivu* came across the place maybe a hundred years afterward and figured it was a gift from the gods. They normally don't live here, but various groups visit for religious ceremonies. But when the big winds blow, many of the people come here for refuge. The trees are very solid; only a couple have fallen in the last fifty years, and none of those during the razor rains. They figure that if they put themselves in God's hands, they'll be safe."

More lightning, another quick view.

"If they've withstood three hundred years of weather, they'll probably withstand this next storm," Zarant said.

Cinch smiled. His grandfather's logic again. But here it was easy to see why the gray men could believe it. These trees were impressive.

"Shit!" Pakita said from behind him.

Cinch turned. "What?"

"I put a squealer on a couple of Lavan's cash accounts. If any substantial money was withdrawn, the computer was set up to send a signal. He just cleared out both of them, several hundred thousand cees each." She waved the com she held.

Cinch turned and looked out at the Root Caves. It would have been interesting to ride out a major hurricane there, but it didn't look like it was going to happen. There were probably a lot of reasons that Lavan might need large amounts of money in a hurry, but Cinch knew the real one: the man was going to run. That, unfortunately, was more interesting than the oncoming razor rains.

Cinch sighed. Well. He didn't have to worry about making his decision about what he was going to do anymore. He was going to have to catch the crooked governor before he got away.

For just a few seconds, he considered pretending he didn't know what the governor was going to do. That he cleaned out a bank account didn't prove anything. No court in the galaxy would convict anybody of anything based on that flimsy bit of information. Maybe he was going to buy a new cart. Maybe he was worried about the banks failing and he was going to put his money into an old sock under his bed. And to tell the truth, if the man left this planet, everybody would be a lot better off and it wouldn't be that much of a loss. A fugitive was not a blot on a ranger's record, not if he had the evidence to put him away.

He shook his head. Nice fantasy, but he knew better.

chapter 26

Lavan chose to drive his sporter through the rainy night, for several reasons. First, it was going to be the last time he got to put the powerful little beast through its paces. Second, because it was fast and he was in a hurry. Third, because it was small and light enough so when he shifted into all-drive mode it would roll over just about any relatively flat area, which meant he could put it on a *sapi* path if need be. He didn't think anybody was going to be looking for him yet, much less in the middle of a howling *wembemvua,* but it was best to play it safe. Things might have gone sour with his original plan but his escape plot was still intact. It was up to him to treat it carefully enough to keep it that way.

He whipped the little craft along the dark and mostly empty streets, his official ID holoproj flashing over the top to keep the traffic cools from stopping him. He felt a little angry. Well, okay, more than a little angry, but just now it was counterproductive to let it out. The other side had certainly gummed up his plans. He hated them for it. Then again, he could hate them just as well over a drink with an expensive woman at a pleasure kiosk on Zöldfú, and it would be a lot safer. Whatever else he considered himself, he was a realist. Someday when he had time, maybe he would put together a way to repay those who had fucked him here. A nice explosive in the ranger's breakfast, maybe, some ground glass for O'thea, a fulminating bacterial infection injected into Zarant to burn his brain out. Pleasant fantasies . . .

An ambulance zipped through the intersection ahead of him at a right angle, siren screaming, red-and-blue lights strobing purple together in the darkness. Now was not the time to indulge revenge fantasies, either. Pay attention to the business at hand. Collect your last bits of baggage from the office and get out of town. The drive to North Base would take six hours, even in the sporter with full floodlamps lit, and that was assuming he got out ahead of the storm. It was not the time to dick around with anything. Already the winds were gusting to sixty, sixty-five klicks, and the main body of the *wembemvua* would be here in the next few hours, did the forecasts have any accuracy. By the time it got this far, he planned to be long gone.

A sheet of plastic blew across the street in front of the sporter, spun into a rough ball despite the harder rain now starting to fall. The sporter's blowers were no longer enough to keep the screen clean by themselves, and he turned the wipers on to sluice away the heavier downpour. It was going to be a rough night for those who stayed here. He would have liked to watch the fury of the tempest from inside the safety of his home. He enjoyed such weather, but if he didn't leave now his travel window might close. It was the mark of a civilized man to know when to leave the party, he'd always believed, and now was most definitely the time.

He dialed the lights up on the sporter. The wind drove the rain aslant and fitfully through the intensified beams, defining the light almost as if it had sharp edges. It seemed almost appropriate, somehow, that he should be leaving in the middle of the arriving storm. Let it wash away his past as it blew through the city. When the storm passed away, he would be gone with it.

"You have a flitter, scooter, something fast I can borrow?"

Zarant nodded at Cinch. "Got a little two-seat flitter. Not as fast as a scooter but it's got a roof. You'll need it in this weather."

"Pakita says he's got a private ship at North Base. If I go there, I might be able to cut him off."

"You sure about this?"

"No. But it makes sense. He gets offworld and intergalactic, we might not ever find him again. If he thinks we've got enough to drydock him, he can stay and fight or he can run. When he pulled the cash out of those accounts, I think he told us which it was going to be."

"You could just let him go," O'thea said.

Cinch nodded. "Yeah, I could. I have to tell you, I thought about it. That would solve your problem, him being gone, no matter how it happened or where he went. But just getting rid of him isn't what they pay me for."

"Nobody here would ever say anything," Zarant said. "Nobody other than us would know."

"I would know," Cinch said. "If I ever leave the ranger business, I want to walk away clean. Can't walk too well with your eyes closed and your fingers in your ears."

Zarant nodded. "We understand that. You need any help?"

"No."

"Okay. K(!)ree will show you where the flitter is stored. Good luck."

"Thanks."

Zarant and O'thea took turns hugging him, and then Cinch hurried away.

Lavan pulled into his private slot and powered the gullwing door on the sporter open. The parking structure was empty, save for a single electric trike and that had probably been left by somebody riding with someone else. Everybody else had been sent home and it gave the place a hollow feeling.

The rain slashed harder at the structure and he could hear the wind tugging at the sharp edges and crannies of it. He started to slide out of the cart. At the last second, he glanced down at the seat and saw his pistol between the seats, where he had shoved it. There had been a time years ago when he'd worn the custom-made gun everywhere. He fancied himself a pretty good shot and had spun fantasies about plugging an assassin in the heart or between the eyes as the villain tried to shoot him. He'd stopped hauling the gun around because it was heavy and inconvenient and because, despite the frontier ambience of the planet, nobody had ever made a serious attempt to assassinate him, not even the cutthroats.

He grinned. He still thought of them that way, even though, as far as he knew, they had never fired a shot except in self-defense.

But here and now, with the storm slapping wet and windy hands against the parking structure hard enough to shake it, he picked up the expensive pistol in its hand-sewn horsehide paddle holster and slipped the formed plastic paddle under the waistband of his pants. The rain jacket he wore draped low enough to cover the holster, hiding it from a casual viewer. He was a fugitive now, and nothing and nobody could get in his way, were he to escape. He had never killed anybody with his own hands, not even in his head-breaking days as a young man, but did that need arise, he was up to it.

He turned and headed for his office.

Cinch looked at the map of Kivu, the backlighting of the small flatscreen casting a dim blue glow inside the flitter. North Base was about as far from where he was as the city of Kiwanda, the top point of a rough and slightly tilted equilateral triangle. There was only one main road from the city to North Base and in places it narrowed to two lanes. If the governor went that way and if Cinch could set up in the right spot, he could see him go by.

Iffy, all right. There was no guarantee that Lavan would take that road. He could just as easily fly, couldn't he? Or go a little farther out of his way and travel by fast boat?

Not likely. Flying in a hurricane was not real bright, nor was going to sea. Of course, he could be halfway there by now, even if he did drive. Best Cinch get his own craft moving.

He cranked the engines, brought the repellors on line, trimmed the fans, and took off.

Lavan's boot heels echoed in the quiet building, sounding quite loud. Inside the effects of the oncoming storm were muted, an occasional gust of wind or rain rattling a window, that was pretty much it. The off-hours lighting was on, though it flickered a couple of times. The building had its own power, of course, but that wouldn't kick in unless the main net went down.

He walked toward his office, using his keycard to open the locked doors in his path. It was eerie, being alone in here. He'd never seen the building so quiet and empty.

When he reached his office and slid the door aside, he discovered, much to his shock, that he wasn't alone in here after all.

Seated behind the governor's desk, grinning, was Munga Vita.

# chapter 27

The storm was arriving faster than the reports said it would. The little flitter rocked in the wind, hit a downdraft once that dropped it two hundred meters in about that many seconds. Cinch kept a steady hand on the controls, his airspeed not half what the computer said the craft would do if pressed. He flew across the wind; it came from the south, his right, mostly, and if it had been a headwind, he would have been traveling a lot more slowly than he was. Still, he was moving, and probably faster than a ground or GE cart would be able to. He had picked out a spot on the map where he hoped to set up a surveillance, a narrowing of the road where it climbed a clear-cut hill through a series of hairpins on the edge of something called The Binatang Wildlife Preserve. With any luck, he would be able to see far enough down the road to notice a vehicle a long way off. He had his spotting scope plugged into the flitter's charger to make sure the batteries in it were fresh when he got there. He hoped he would get there before Lavan did.

If Lavan were coming this way at all.

There was the risk. He might not be. All Cinch had to go on was his instinct and that had failed him before. Not too often, but enough so he was not certain. Damned expectations again.

No, he couldn't depend on it. But if he were pushed, he would bet his pension on it. Lavan was going to run this way. No doubt at all.

"Munga!"

"Surprise, surprise," the redhead said, smiling. "I knew you'd show up here before the storm hit too hard. You got the look of a man going somewhere, is that right?"

On Lavan's desk in front of Vita lay a pistol. The same pistol the governor had given him, without a doubt, only the grips on it were not the faux ivory ones with the explosive in them. He wondered what happened. Knowing Vita, he would find out soon.

Sure enough, Vita caught the look. He said, "Just how stupid do you think I am, Yogen? I mean, you crapped all over me for the last few months and then you up and give me this beautiful piece out of the kindness of your soul?"

"I don't know what you mean," Lavan said evenly. "What are you talking about?"

"I'm talking about a fucking bomb hidden in the handles of the gun you gave me! Set to go up when I pushed the switch that took down the jail!"

"That's the same jail you blew apart after I told you not to do it?"

Vita laughed. "That's right. I figured I didn't work for you no more when I found the little extra present you included. It was the door scanner in the police station that did it, you know. Fluoroproj showed the stuff in the grips nice as you please. I guess you weren't thinking too well when you did that."

Lavan didn't say anything. Vita *was* as stupid as he thought. It was an accident the explosives had been spotted, but he also didn't think this was the time to say so. Instead, he said, "So what now?"

"Well, I planned to kill you. But then I realized, hey,

what would that accomplish? You'd be dead and I'd feel a little better, but so what? Maybe it would be better, I thought, if I just ... retired. You know, just gave up all this mercenary shit and went away. But to do that, I need a little more cushion. I thought that instead of killing you, I'd have you supply it, then we could part and go our own ways. You tried to kill me, I tried to do you, we're even and no hard feelings. How does that sound?"

Vita looked relaxed, leaning back in the chair. He had to know he could shift just a little and get to his pistol before Lavan could take two steps. Not that he would think he would need the gun. Lavan knew as well as Vita that the bigger man could snap his neck with his hands easily enough. In his position—with his brain—the governor would think he was in control, too.

"That's it? I give you money and you leave?"

"You give me lots of money. A million, say. Then I leave."

*Lying like a storehouse full of cheap rugs,* Lavan thought. *The second I hand it over, he'll shoot me. Probably somewhere painful but not immediately fatal so he can watch me die slowly. He might as well be wearing a flashing sign promising it.*

"All right. I don't want any trouble," Lavan said.

"That's what I thought you'd say. Basically when you get right down to it, you're not much of a man, are you, Yogen? A coward, isn't that right? As long as you have somebody else to do your fighting for you, you're fine, but when it comes down to blooding your own knife, you got the backbone of a slug."

"Right," Lavan said, as he reached back and pulled his pistol from its holster and brought it up to bear on Vita. He moved slowly and smoothly so as not to alarm him. Vita didn't expect his victim to be strapped, that was plain to see; the big man's expression turned to surprise and fear as he realized what Lavan was doing. Finally.

He lunged for the gun on the desk.

Lavan shot him. From three meters, it was easy to put the bullet square in his heart. When Vita fell back in the chair, he fired another round, just for the hell of it.

It hit Vita right between his stupid fucking eyes.

Cinch found the place he wanted and it was not quite as good as he hoped but not bad. There was a buffer zone of smallish trees on the switchback, enough to mostly hide the flitter. Beyond those, the jungle was as thick as any he'd seen.

From here he could see two loops of the road down the hillside. If he caught a vehicle climbing on the lower loop, he'd have time to put the scope on it for maybe ten seconds or so when it reached the next curve. Should be enough time to see who was driving, all things going well.

He set up the scope, put the starlight attachment on it, and trained it on the lower curve of the two-lane road. He'd seen only a few vehicles traveling the road on his flight in, and while the wind wasn't as strong here as it had been at the Root Caves, it was picking up.

He hoped he wasn't too late.

Lavan reholstered his pistol and stared at the body sprawled in his chair. There wasn't anybody around who could have heard the shots. Probably that trike in the garage belonged to Vita. *Had* belonged to Vita.

He shoved the body aside and thumbprinted his desk's lock open. Inside he removed the three small treasures he had come to collect. There was the fist-sized strawberry crystal from Arbai, worth a hundred thousand cees. Next to that was the antique chronometer his mother had given him on his twenty-first birthday. It was an ancient LED Pulsar, probably worth a few hundred cees or maybe less, but it had personal meaning. Finally there was the statuette of the hand dancer, sitting with her wrists crossed, looking enigmatic. She was carved from black opal, easily worth half a million. He didn't plan to part with any of these items, but if need be, the crystal and statuette could be converted to cash. He owned them under one of his fake names and the bills of sale were perfectly valid. The artworks were beautiful and valuable and he had never shown either to anyone, so nobody knew the governor owned them.

He pulled his expanding briefcase from the bottom drawer and carefully put the chronometer, crystal, and statuette inside. *There.*

He took a last look around before he left. A lot of good memories here, but they were spoiled a little by Vita's body. Ah, well. That was how it went. Always a fly in the ointment somewhere.

He turned and left, put it all behind him. He did not look back.

Cinch left the flitter after a couple of hours, to pee and to stretch. He drank from the water bottle he'd brought, though dying of thirst wasn't likely to be a problem once the hurricane got here. The wind grew stronger, gusting hard enough to sway the trees and rearrange his hair as he slid back into the flitter's seat. No rain yet, but he could smell it coming. The night had an anticipatory feel to it, the impending storm promising to be memorable.

Twice long-haul vans had rolled past, one going toward, one coming from the direction of the city. Neither of the drivers had noticed him parked in the trees, or if they did, had given no sign of it. He heard them talking on the open opchan band of the flitter's radio, and it was truckers' jive, all about road conditions and locations. He also caught part of a 'cast from a long way off, a bounce from a driver halfway around the continent, well away from the approaching *wembemvua.*

It was hot where this driver was, and he'd had a climb out and clear his windscreen twice in the last three hours, all the dead bugs in the summer night musta hit his truck.

Cinch grinned wryly at the trucker. What would it be

like to have nothing more to worry about than cleaning dead insects off your windscreen? Probably not much compared to waiting for a major criminal to pass by so you could detain him. There was a time when he would have thought such work incredibly dull, driving a truck. Now? Now he wasn't so sure.

The wind blew and the rain arrived, fitfully at first, big drops spattering in noisy waves, stopping, then returning. After a few minutes, the rain settled into a steady thrum on the flitter's roof. He was glad he'd taken this vehicle and not the cycle. Being outside in the downpour would have been miserable, even covered in osmotic hoop film. He'd spent too many hours on too many worlds sitting surveillance in the rain to think it anything like glorious. All those entcom vids where the rangers kicked in doors and blasted the villains into red goo were fairly silly. Sure, he'd shot a few people over the years—well, maybe more than a few, but it was relative—he'd worked thousands of cases and had pulled a weapon in maybe a hundred, actually shot a gun in fewer than twenty of those investigations. Most of the time the glory of rangering was like this: sitting alone in a cart or under a bush in the dark or the rain, or both, somewhere, waiting. Or footwork, asking questions, gathering data, assembling it like pieces of a puzzle. If his actual work had been as eventful as the entcoms projjed it, he'd have probably been dead fifteen years by now.

Lavan had planned to leave the sporter and use one of his personal flitters for the trip to the port, but when he emerged from the building, the rainfall was torrential, the wind blowing hard enough to twist road signs and rock the sporter as he drove. Not good flying weather, especially in a low-altitude flitter. One hard downdraft and he'd be plowing a field with his face. No, might as well stay in the sporter. It was fast, fully fueled, and low-slung enough to keep to its wheels when the wind tried to grab it.

He had nothing else to collect. The pouch on the seat next to him held his new start, his treasures were nestled safely in the briefcase on the floor. He had his gun. Not as much as he would have liked, but certainly something to show for his tenure as governor. The party was nearly over and it was time to beat the rush and leave. There was nothing more to hold him here.

He had regrets, of course, but not so many that he would lose any sleep over them. Life surprised him now and then and he didn't much care for surprises, unless he was passing them out. But—what was to be done? You had to deal with the reality, he had learned that over the years, no matter how much you didn't like it.

Another day, he would allow himself the luxury to stew about chances missed and efforts wasted. Truth was, he couldn't really complain. He would be better off than ninety-nine percent of the whole galaxy if he never earned another cent and how bad could that be?

Drive on, Yogen, and smile. You really don't have any worries.

With his ID flashing, the governor turned north and headed out of town.

# chapter 28

Cinch checked the load in his pistol's gas-powered magazine. It carried six starfish rounds, good for soft targets. He didn't really think he would need the weapon. Lavan was a smooth hand, much more likely to use a computer than a gun. Still, Cinch had been a ranger long enough to know he shouldn't take anything for granted. He wanted the man alive and on a judge's sentencing dock, sweating and pale as he waited for the ax to fall. The governor would run if he thought there was danger, but he didn't seem like the type to stand and fight.

Of course, Cinch had been wrong before. He had an old bullet wound on the inside of his left leg, the scar deliberately left unrevised by the surgeon's laser to remind him not to assume anything. Shove him into a corner hard and narrow enough and the most cowardly man will sometimes turn into a berserker.

Well. If the storm didn't block the road with a fallen tree or a blown-over building, maybe they'd see how Lavan reacted when he saw Cinch. If he were headed this way. If Cinch didn't miss him.

If.

Lavan cleared the city in about ten minutes. There was a lot more traffic coming into Kiwanda, even from the north, than there was leaving it. With good reason: For the last sixty years, the city's structures had been built with *wembemvua* in mind. Until a couple of years ago, some of the smaller bedroom communities didn't have nearly so strict a building code. Those same communities had screamed in outrage when he'd signed the legislation requiring all new structures to meet planetary codes modeled on those of the city. He would bet half his fortune that those who had built legally since were glad of it this night. There had been, as always, those independent spirits who refused to listen to their government. There were plenty of those among the First and even the last wave who sneaked around, forged permissions and inspections and built substandard offices and homes. Those who did it while laughing behind their hands at the legislature and governor who obviously didn't know shit. They didn't know that most of the crooked inspectors were on Lavan's payroll. That much of the money they spent cheating the government went into one of his accounts anyway. Many of those hardshell anarchists would have their flimsy houses picked apart by the wind's claws in the next few hours. They would wish they had listened to him.

People were so stupid. You try to do something for their own good and they hate you for it.

Lavan grinned. It was easy to smile on someone's misfortune if they refused to heed your warnings of it. It served them right.

All in all, he'd been a good governor, as good as any the planet had ever had. Sure, he'd filled his pockets, but so what? That was a small perk, nobody got hurt by it, and the planet had prospered, hadn't it? It was so fucking unfair that the rangers had come down on him. True, he had called them in, but he hadn't really believed they would find anything to cause him trouble.

Well. You live and you learn. And right now, he was going to live somewhere else and learn other things. Fuck this world and fuck the Stellar Rangers. He was gone.

# chapter 29

The storm opened wide its maw and swallowed the jungle. The rain washed over Cinch's flitter, found a place where the window sealant had either been badly applied or had finally given up the fight. A trickle meandered down the inside of the window, a tiny stream that branched and sent a pair of rivulets into the floor's padding. That was the least of his worries. The rain and wind combined cut his vision to a few meters. if somebody come up the hill, he hoped they had their headlamps dialed all the way to full brightness.

Somewhere past midnight, with the storm till building, Cinch's personal com chirped.

He picked it up. "Yeah?"

"Having fun out there, ranger?" Chayne O'thea.

He was glad she called. The angry *wembemvua* was not particularly good company.

"Oh, yeah, I'm enjoying myself a whole bunch. Tell your husband he gave me a leaky flitter."

"It's raining where you are? We're having a nice balmy night here."

Cinch heard the wind in the background, howling from the com's speaker.

"That right?"

"Well. Maybe a little drizzle. Looks like the eye will pass about thirty klicks southeast of here in the next few minutes. We've lost one tree, nobody hurt. Any sign of your quarry yet?"

"No."

The conversation was, as usual, scrambled. Anybody who tried to fly here to check on him if they could unscramble the com deserved to die. So he said, "I'm on the edge of The Binatang Wildlife Preserve, still waiting. Not a lot of traffic out this way."

"Better keep your doors locked. There are some big felines and ursines in the preserve. Also some of our people live there."

*"Majivu?"*

"And humans, too. Laird sent them after the last fight we had with Vita's thugs. There are caves there, real caves. The storm won't bother them."

Before he could say anything else, a faint gleam of light filtered through the cascade running down the flitter's windscreen.

"Got to go. I think I've got company here."

"Be careful, Cinch."

He shut the com off and shoved it back into his belt. He looked through the spookeye scope at the second bend in the road. The scope's LG imager was set on high, the magnification low to give him a better field of view.

There. There was a cart climbing the hill. Cinch mostly saw the line of headlamps on the front, a phosphor smear that left ghostly trails. The rain was a mixed blessing. It made it a lot harder to see anything; then again, it slowed considerably the cart's progress up the rise, the only reason he managed to spot it at all. He didn't think much of the idea of letting Lavan get past him—if this was Lavan—then having to chase him in this deluge. Probably a good way to get them both killed.

Was this his quarry? He hadn't been able to see the driver's face. Could be anybody in that cart, a small vehicle, looked like a two-seater. It wasn't a good night for a leisurely drive in the country, but there could be myriad reasons why that little cart was climbing this little hill just at the moment, none of them having anything to do with Cinch or Lavan.

Well. Better safe than sorry. He was going to have to get wet.

He'd already hoop-filmed his gear. It had been awkward in the flitter, coating things with the clear osmotic film. For a few hours, his gun, his com, and his other belt equipment would be extra-waterproof. And he'd managed to make a couple of passes over his hat, though he didn't think that was going to do him much good. If it didn't blow off and strangle him with the chin strap, the angle of the incoming rain would easily blow under the hat's wide brim.

Cinch took a couple of deep breaths and relaxed as much as he could, then started the flitter's engine. A few seconds later, he idled the little craft forward and parked it across the road, blocking part of both lanes. He shut the engines down, took another breath, and opened the door.

The wind and rain slashed at him, bent the brim of his hat down on one side, and soaked the left side of his clothes before he got the door closed again. He crouched, the wind trying to shove him over, and started working his way down the slope. He had his spookeyes on, dialed off and clear to protect his eyes, but the rain streamed over the lenses and made them worse than useless. He shoved the eyes up and blinked away the rain as best he could.

The road curved away and down slightly about fifty meters from where he left the cart. Somebody rounding the curve would see the parked flitter there. On a clear night, moving at speed, a driver would probably hit the flitter or have to leave the road to get around it. On a night like tonight, a sane driver would be moving a lot slower, so he'd have plenty of time to stop. If it were Cinch, he wouldn't want to swing wide and risk the wet shoulder at any kind of speed, so he'd creep around the flitter even if he wasn't curious enough to stop and check it out.

If somebody else was at the controls of the cart, Cinch was going to have to apologize. Carefully. Out here on the road in the middle of the night in the middle of a hurricane, a driver could be armed and skittish. If Cinch came running up out of nowhere waving his own pistol, he could get shot and nobody would blame the driver.

Well, shit, I was driving along in the middle of a fucking *wembemvua* and there's this flitter sitting in the middle of the fucking road and then this guy holding a fucking gun makes a run at me. What am I supposed to do? Wait until he fucking *shot* me before I did anything?

No, if it wasn't Lavan, Cinch would flash a light and make a lot of noise from a fair way off before he did any explaining.

He reached the spot he wanted, completely soaked, and squatted next to a small stand of thigh-thick trees on the drive's side of the road. As the cart swung around the curve, the lights would shine mostly across the road; he should be practically invisible here.

The wind tried to pull his hat off. He kept his left hand pressing down on the crown, even though the brim flapped like the wings of a demented bird. He kept his right hand near the butt of his pistol.

Lavan was tired and once again angry. The drive had been a trial. The storm had blown in faster than expected and thrown crap at him all the way out of the city. A piece of somebody's roof had nearly smacked into him, bouncing across the road like a child's ball. Three times he had driven around trees that blocked part of the highway. He'd passed a number of carts and vans parked on the roadside, drivers and passengers huddled inside, probably too scared to move. There had been a smoldering wreck at an intersection a few kilometers outside Kiwanda, a collision between a trike and a food wagon. The trike was smashed almost flat and burned a wet black. The wagon had fallen onto its side and trays of sandwiches and pastries lay all around, turned into soggy mush by the rain. He hadn't seen any bodies.

It had taken nearly an hour to drive a distance that normally would have been covered in five minutes.

Finally he was out of the grid and on the more or less open road. He couldn't outrace the storm, though, and the drive had been slowed because of it. It wouldn't do to wind up in a ditch or wrapped around a tree because he hit a slick patch at speed and lost control of the sporter. The little cart mostly shrugged off the effects of the storm as long as it was pulling a tailwind. When the road curved and Lavan had to drive at a right angle to it, the not-so-gentle breeze rocked the sporter, even as low to the ground as it was. Once on a hairpin when he was driving directly into the wind, he had to slow to a walk because the blowers and wipers together couldn't keep the screen clear enough for him to see more than a few meters ahead.

Even so he was well away from the city. Coming up on the game preserve.

He kept his emergency opchan open and the sporter's radio was full of disaster teams calling each other, hospitals directing ambulance transports, fire and police officials dispatching units to various storm-caused disasters. They might be looking for the governor to tell him what was going on, but they wouldn't be looking for him halfway to North Base.

Almost free.

So he arrived there a few hours later than he'd planned. It didn't matter. The storm would blow itself out over land, turn into fitfull squalls and a lot of rain, and in a day or so, soon as the winds died down, he would be on his ship and offplanet. While whoever they put in charge was worrying about cleaning up after the *wembemvua*, Lavan would be on a starliner heading for a pleasure kiosk. By the time the city regained its equilibrium, he would be enjoying the rarest wines, the hottest women, and the most exquisite food money could buy. Maybe he'd offer them a silent toast . . .

He rounded a curve as he climbed a small hill and saw a flitter parked in the middle of the road. Across the middle of the road.

Shit!

He slowed the cart, came to a stop ten meters away from the flitter. His lights were sufficient to light the craft brightly, even through the thick waves of rain that coned the beams. Unless somebody was lying down in the flitter, it was empty.

What had happened here? Why would a flitter be parked out in the middle of nowhere across the road this way? Some kind of freak accident?

Of a moment the reason hit him.

It was a trap!

Because he had his foot on the cart's brake, the stoplamps on the cart's rear were lit. The red glow of the lamps wasn't much against the hard rain, but it was enough for him to see in his mirror the man running up behind him.

A man with a gun in his hand—

Cinch saw it was Lavan from the cart's instrument glow as he went past, slowing to a stop thirty or forty meters away. He came up, drew his pistol, and started running toward the cart. If he were lucky and fast enough, he could get to the cart before Lavan had a clue about what was happening. It didn't look like the sporter's windows were bulletproof and even if they were, Lavan couldn't know if Cinch had AP rounds in the pistol. With the muzzle of a gun pointed almost in your ear, you wouldn't want to risk it. Even if the governor had a gun, Cinch would have the advantage. If he moved wrong, Cinch would shoot.

But when he was still ten meters away, the brake lights

went off and the wheels spun on the wet road as the cart accelerated suddenly. He must have seen him—!

He almost made it.

He pointed the cart toward the left side of the road and slewed that way, but the traction was bad and the cart's rear end swung wide as it rounded the flitter's front end. The cart's rear wheels went off the road and hit soft ground, ground turned into mud by the driving rain. What traction there was vanished from the cart's rear. The front wheels tried to pull the sporter back onto the road but it was wet, too, and the result was a pivot, a skid that threw the little cart to his left and completely onto the muddy shoulder. For a moment, the sporter slid sideways, then backwards. It stopped when the rear end smashed into a small tree. Lavan pressed the accelerator down. Too hard. The tires dug through the mud, making that unique *reennnhh!* sound as the cart settled to the axles.

Like a fly stuck in tree sap, the cart was mired and unable to escape.

It was an instant realization and Lavan did not hesitate a second longer worrying about it. He grabbed his pistol and the bag of gems and platinum and bailed out. He fell in the mud, slid two meters in it down the slope. Then he was up and running, nearly blind from the wind and rain, slogging through calf-deep mud toward the edge of the forest.

Cinch watched the sporter try to sweep around the flitter, saw that Lavan couldn't hold it. The cart cut a swath through the muddy shoulder, and stopped against a tree.

He had him now.

Cinch ran toward the cart.

But the door gullwinged opposite him. The cart was turned sideways to his viewpoint, between him and the driver. The cart's lights lit the sky, showing sheets of rain gusting through their beams.

Cinch slipped as he hit the mud, went to one knee, slid that way for half a meter before he regained his feet. By the time he rounded the stuck cart, Lavan was halfway to the trees.

For a second, he thought about shooting. There was a time when he might have done that, but lately, he had mellowed some. Yes, he had shot the thugs attacking the village, but they had been armed and ready to kill him. The governor was on foot, panicked, running. How far could he get?

Cinch looked at the cart. It was stuck pretty good, he wouldn't bet on its moving under its own power until the mud dried, and maybe not then. He could barely see the tops of the tires. He aimed, fired twice. It only took a second to shoot a hole in each of the tires facing him. They were probably self-sealers, but the exit holes were fist-sized and they weren't going to seal those. Nobody was driving the sporter anywhere without a lot of work first.

Then he turned and ran after Lavan.

The governor was panicked. It was the fucking ranger! He hadn't seen him clearly, but who else could it be? Vita was dead and it wasn't Zarant, he hadn't been big enough. He was sure it was the ranger and not some enterprising thief playing at highway robbery in the storm. He didn't believe in coincidences that large. Not now, not here. Somehow the ranger had figured out where he was going. Somehow he had set this up.

A distant lightning flash illuminated the trees for an instant. That happened during *wembemvua,* the big storms generated all kinds of weather on their own. Tornadoes that ran before the wind; thunder cells, sometimes with ball lightning that fell and rolled on the ground before exploding; hail; even snow.

*Worry about the goddamned weather later, Yogen. Right now you've got to get away from the ranger.*

He made it to the trees, slowed, and risked a look backward.

There the ranger came. Another electrical flash confirmed it. It was Carston.

He was forty meters back, easily, but Lavan whipped up the pistol and snapped off two shots. He couldn't see if the bullets hit anything, but the muzzle flash was a brilliant yellow-orange tongue of fire that blinded him.

*Shit!*

Cinch saw the muzzle blast forty meters down the slope and in the trees. He didn't hear the shots for the wind and rain, but he dropped flat into a sheet of muddy water. Too late, of course, the bullets would have already beaten his reaction time. But he didn't feel any impacts as he came up to a half-assed *seiza* position and returned the fire, two quick shots in the general direction of the afterimage printed on his retinas. So much for sparing the poor frightened governor. The man was a shooter, a surprise, but there it was. Of course at that range and in this weather, it would have been a miracle if he'd hit anything. Even so, he had tried. So the gloves came off now.

He stood and half slid, half skipped down the hillside.

The ranger shot back. Lavan saw the fire from his gun. One of the bullets hit a tree not twenty centimeters to the right of his head, close enough for him to hear it and feel something splatter from the tree into the side of his neck.

Lavan spun and ran.

Cinch reached the trees. He had a flashlight in his belt but he hesitated to use it. In the darkness, a bright light would make him too easy a target.

The storm did that for him when a jagged bolt of cloud-to-cloud lightning forked overhead, pulsing for a brief moment of near daylight. The thunder was loud enough to get past the wind and rain and, from the time it took to reach him, not far away.

He saw Lavan and crouched lower, but the man was running and not interested in shooting. The thinned trees this close to the road seemed to join into a wall of wood just in front of Lavan where the ground leveled off.

Once he got in there, it would be a bitch following him.

Cinch was a pretty good tracker. He could read trail sign, had learned from his grandfather who had learned from his grandfather who had learned it from a native Amerind on Earth. But finding trail sign in a jungle, in the dark, during a hurricane, well, that might be beyond even his grandfather's grandfather's skills. It was sure as hell likely to be outside Cinch's range.

He started after Lavan. Yeah, the man wasn't going to get far on foot in this weather, but then again, it was a big fucking jungle and there were a lot of places to hide. It could be a long night.

Lavan ran blindly until he hit a tree with his left shoulder hard enough to spin him around. *Ow, shit!*

He fell, hit a prickly bush on the way down. He scrabbled up. He couldn't see where he was going; he'd beat himself to death if he kept running.

Okay, okay, he had to settle down. The ranger couldn't see him, he was invisible. All he had to do was turn, go at an angle for a while, then change direction. He didn't have to run, he could go as slow as he wanted—

More lightning, followed by almost immediate thunder. Plenty bright enough to cast shadows. Bright enough to read by.

Bright enough for somebody to *see* him if they happened to look in the right direction.

Okay, so he had to move a little faster than slow, he was still in good shape. He had a gun, he had his money—the artwork was still in the cart, but that was not a problem—he was going to have to circle around and get back to the sporter sooner or later. The cart was probably locked into the mud, but the flitter was still there. Sure, the ranger probably had the keycard but Lavan knew the police emergency override code for commercial vehicles, he could start the thing. Keep it low, a meter or two off the ground, that way even if the wind knocked it down, it wouldn't do much damage, he could millimeter along, baby it, get far enough away so the ranger couldn't catch him.

Of course, the ranger might expect him to do something like that, he'd have to be careful, but this was only a setback, he wasn't caught, wasn't done yet.

The trees around him swayed under the storm's pounding, howled and whistled in many voices. Leaves and branches fell with the rain. He worried that he'd be crushed by a falling limb; that would be a terrible irony. Millions of cees worth of precious metal and stones in his hand lying in the mud after he was flattened by a damned tree. It would be so . . . senseless.

It would be easy to get lost in here. He couldn't go too far into the preserve before he started his circle back to the road. He could use the wind for direction—it was coming from the south—it would be simple. First he would keep it at his left, then behind him, then at his right, and he'd make a squared-off loop and be heading back for the road. Go a klick in each direction, maybe, that should do it. It would be all right if he just kept moving.

Cinch found the trail, much to his own amazement. There were plenty of branches down, leaves stuck gluelike to everything, but he came to a flattened bush, branches snapped in a way that said something heavy had fallen on it. Only there wasn't anything heavy there now. When he risked a quick flash of his belt light, shielding it with his cupped hand as best he could, he saw a footprint in the leafy muck next to the broken bush.

Lavan had fallen here. Gotten up, and headed off that way.

Cinch rose from his crouch, water pouring from the hat brim in streams. This was lucky, but ultimately no good. He'd never be able to follow him for any distance. As soon as Lavan took another tack, that would be it. He couldn't depend on his leaving any more obvious clues.

The smart thing would be to go back to the flitter. On foot in the jungle, sooner or later Lavan would realize the futility of his flight. He couldn't walk to civilization from here, certainly not tonight. He wasn't equipped for a trek through a hurricane—who was?—and he'd have to know the only way to escape would be to secure transportation.

There wasn't any transportation in the jungle, only back on the road. The sporter. The flitter. Maybe a passing truck, although with the wind getting stronger by the minute, probably not much chance of the latter. If Lavan had any sense, he'd have to have figured that out.

The rational man in Cinch's mind told him this, urged him to turn around and go back to the road, to set up another trap on the flitter and wait. He could disable the flitter's electronics, pull a circuit chip so it wouldn't go no matter what, and wait. It wouldn't be comfortable in the rain, but he was miserable anyway. That was the logical, reasonable thing to do.

The hunter in Cinch told the rational man to fuck off. He was close, he could almost smell his prey. A few more minutes and he would have him. *Push on, Cinch, don't quit now! Staple that sucker, make him understand that he's broken the cardinal rule: Don't mess with the Stellar Rangers!*

*Okay,* Cinch compromised with himself. *Here's the deal. I'll try to find him for another ten minutes. If I don't see him or some undeniable sign of him, I go back.*

That didn't make either the rational man or the hunter happy, but that was too bad. They'd have to live with it.

\* \* \*

The wind blew harder, even though the rain seemed to slacken some. The electrical pod moved off, giving Lavan fewer and dimmer flashes. He didn't know how far he'd gone and he decided to hell with it, he was going to put the wind at his back and start his return toward the road.

Lucky thing, too. A big tree crashed down to his left once he put the wind at his back, right about where he would have been if he'd kept going deeper into the jungle. He felt it shake the ground, felt the force of it vibrate in his chest when the trunk hit.

He stopped to catch his breath, leaned against a tree bigger around than three men, a tree that had to be a couple of centuries old. Other *wembemvua* had passed through its crown in those centuries and still it stood. Maybe it would last long enough to keep him from being blown away for one more storm.

Five minutes, he told himself. That'll be plenty.

The gusts at his back pressed him toward the thick trunk. How hard would the wind be if all those trees weren't blocking it, fragmenting it, slowing it down?

A crosswind came at him from his left, surprising him. He was braced wrong and it nearly shoved him off-balance. An odd current bouncing off the woods.

But as he stood there, more of the crosswinds began to play against him. The rain slackened yet more, but the wind didn't decrease, and it wasn't just a few gusts, it was now blowing steadily from that direction.

The wind had shifted.

Jesus. What did that mean?

What was that going to do to his sense of direction?

Worse, what might it have already done to his sense of direction? How could that happen?

The answer slapped him almost as hard as the gale.

It's a circular storm. It whirls around a center. And that center must be moving toward him instead of passing in a parallel track south and east of him as it was supposed to have done.

Shit. He'd better turn toward the road while he could still figure it out and keep moving in a straight line!

Cinch felt the wind shift and the rain slacken. He remembered the hurricane he had gone through with his grandfather all those years ago. The eye. The eye was coming this way. It might only be a few kilometers across, fifty, eighty, and he needed to think about getting back to the flitter. He hadn't left a locator in the vehicle, not thinking he was going for a walk in the jungle when he'd stepped out into the storm, but he was pretty sure he could find his way back to the road. He had always had a good sense of direction, he seldom got lost. Even with the shifting wind, he had a feeling that the road was *that* way. Besides, if the eye did pass overhead, he could find enough of a clear spot to see the stars and he knew he could get a fix that way. A good ranger always learned the star patterns in the hemisphere in which he found himself on a new planet, that was just common sense. They had a pole star here that would give him enough to get a rough idea of north.

*What about Lavan?* the hunter wanted to know.

*He isn't going to escape,* Cinch told the petulant voice in his head. *When he comes back to the flitter—*

*—If he comes back to the flitter,* the hunter said.

*Fine, if. If he does, we'll get him there.*

*Can we shoot him?*

*Jesus.*

Lavan realized he had no idea where he was. The screaming winds tore at him, he was wet, leaves blew all over him. This was hell.

Then, abruptly, the wind went still.

It was almost that fast. One second there was a steady breeze, then next, almost nothing. A few gusts batted at him, then the calm was so quiet he thought maybe for a second that he had gone deaf. His ears popped and when he looked up through the ragged and torn canopy of trees, he saw the night sky. Saw the stars.

It was the eye of the *wembemvua*. He had never experienced one but he recognized it for what it was.

This was his chance. And he knew what to do. He would climb this big tree. Get high enough to see over the tops of the smaller trees, spot the road or the cleared area, a hill, something, then head that way. He probably only had a few minutes, so he had better get moving.

He tucked the pistol into his belt, tied the sack with the coins and gems in it to his belt, and started to climb.

It was going to be all right. He was going to make it out of here. The gods had played a nasty joke, but then they'd given him a reprieve.

Cinch was on his way back toward where he figured the flitter was when he heard a scream. A human voice, he was sure. It was off to his left. He turned and angled toward it, working his way through the thick brush, detouring around fallen trees. This wood was in for a shock when the wind started up again, from the other direction.

He saw the road, or where it had to be, and it was no more than half a klick away. Lavan breathed deeply in relief as he clambered down the tree bole. He'd torn his pants and shirt both during the climb, but that didn't matter. New clothes were cheap.

He was almost on the ground when the big cat stepped out of the darkness and growled at him. It was a liger, easily three meters long from fangs to tail, probably two hundred kilos heavy.

He screamed.

The cat jumped, then bared teeth as long as Lavan's fingers at him, hissing as it did so. It gathered itself to spring, tail twitching.

Lavan fumbled for the gun, got it out. He pointed it at the cat and started firing—

\* \* \*

Cinch heard the shooting. Sounded as if it were no more than fifty or sixty meters away. A handgun. Three, four, five shots—

Hanging on to a wet tree and shooting with one hand, Lavan expected to miss the cat. He was hoping the noise and light flashes would scare it away. The muzzle blasts fogged his sight, leaving him with throbbing purple afterimages but the sharp teeth of the cat did not find him through his impaired vision. When he managed to look to one side, his peripheral gaze picked up the liger lying on its side. He'd hit it, and it must have been a fatal shot, for the animal growled once, shivered, then lay still.

*Thank God!*

He lost his grip and fell, but he was only a couple of meters up and the wet ground cushioned his impact. He got to his feet and looked down at the liger. It was dead enough. He kicked it.

"Freeze!" somebody yelled.

He spun, saw the ranger standing a few meters away, his gun pointed at him. Without thinking, Lavan thrust his pistol out and fired. The gun went off twice and then clicked empty.

But the ranger was falling—

Cinch hesitated, puzzled by what he saw. Lavan, kicking a lion or something like it on the ground. Was he crazy? He yelled at the governor to freeze, but the man spun and fired, so fast! The bullet hit Cinch under the left arm, burned along his ribs and punched through his lat. He felt it leave his back. He spun away from the impact and instinctively reached over with his right hand to grab at the wound. He lost his pistol in the process.

Why hadn't he shot? Lavan had been fast, but not that fast.

He dropped, holding on to the burning spot on his rib.

It went numb even as he hit the wet ground, splashing into a puddle. His gun was gone—

Lavan saw the ranger go down and felt a blast of triumph. He got him! It was over! He only had to get back to the road and he was safe! Did he have any more ammunition for his gun? He would have to reload to shoot the ranger again, to be sure. But it was in the sporter; he hadn't brought any extra. The ranger's gun. He'd dropped it. Where was it?

Cinch looked for his pistol, didn't see it. It must have fallen in the puddle somewhere. He felt around for it, his hand swirling the muddy water.
He heard something growl.
But the cat was dead, wasn't it? It sure looked that way; he could see it and it was not moving.
The growl came again.

Lavan heard the beast rumble and turned to stare at it. How could that be? It was dead, wasn't it? Look, there it was, bloody and flattened, not breathing, not moving. How could it growl?
Then he realized the noise was coming from *behind* him.
Was it the ranger—?
He turned back around.

Cinch saw the big cat edge from behind a tree, tail lashing. It was bigger than the one on the ground, darker, had a thicker mane. He blinked, understanding.
The dead cat's mate.
Lavan's face lit with terror.
The cat leaped.

Lavan swung the empty gun like a club but it didn't slow the cat. The animal hit him, knocked him down. Bit his face. Clawed with its back feet at his belly.
He screamed—

* * *

"Shit!" Cinch swept his hand over the floor of the puddle. Where the fuck was his pistol—?

Lavan's scream was a pulsed series of wordless bleats. *Ah! Ah! Ah!* Then they stopped.

Cinch heard the sounds of small bones being crunched as the cat chewed part of the governor's face off. The white beard turned dark with blood.

His scrabbling hand touched metal. His pistol!

He pulled the gun out of the water, shook it hard to clear the barrel.

The movement caught the cat's attention. It turned and noticed him. Roared and crouched, the governor forgotten.

Cinch pointed the pistol at the cat. It was three meters away, it could cover that ground in one jump, half a second. He better not miss or he was dead—

The cat jumped, but—

It was upward and to one side and not at Cinch. It was as if it had been stung on the rump by an insect. It roared, then jumped again, twisting the other way.

Cinch watched, amazed.

The cat turned and stared at him. It looked puzzled. Then it blinked and fell over.

What the hell—?

Three forms appeared like gray ghosts.

*Majivu.* Carrying blowguns.

What were they—? Oh, yeah. Chayne had told him. Some of the People were here. Now he knew what had happened to the cat.

One of the gray men came and squatted next to Cinch. The *majivu* looked familiar but Cinch didn't know his name. "C(!)arston. Water man." The *majivu* grinned.

Because he was tired and shot, it took Cinch a second to get it. Water man? Oh. The child he'd saved.

The gray man helped him get up. He leaned on the *majivu* and walked over to where the governor lay. The other two *majivu* looked down at the bloody Lavan. Cinch saw that he was badly mauled. His face was a ruin, his intestines had been torn out through a jagged rent in his abdomen. But he was alive. He saw the man raise one arm, a feeble gesture, and he groaned.

Damn. Alive.

He wondered if the gray men here knew who Lavan was. That this ruin on the ground was the one responsible for killing them like cattle and trying to steal their heritage.

One of the gray men lifted his blowgun to his lips and pointed it at the wounded governor.

"Hey," Cinch began, "don't—"

The *majivu* blew. The dart hit the governor's forehead. *Jesus—!*

The other two *majivu* spat on Lavan as he convulsed, then lay still.

"K(!)iller man," the *majivu* supporting Cinch said. "D(!)ead man."

That answered his question. They knew who Lavan was. Who he had been.

chapter **30**

With the chem the medic pumped into him and the tissue culture injected into the bullet wound, Cinch felt almost good. He wouldn't be doing any marathon chin-up sessions for a while, but then again, he wouldn't be doing that if he hadn't been shot.

In the bright morning, with the dregs of the hurricane long blown past the city, he stood next to the transport that would take him to the spaceport. Able to walk the streets of Kiwanda for the first time in many months, Zarant and O'thea stood next to him. The emergency session of the legislature convened after the *wembemvua* finished stomping its way through the country had taken Cinch's report to heart. Lavan was dead and nobody here wanted galactic authorities pissed off at them. The crimes of which the cutthroats stood accused would be investigated carefully, but the local government was more than happy to allow the unofficial ambassador to the *majivu* and his wife to be free on their own bond until these matters could be straightened out. And, they assured Cinch, certainly the charges would be mitigated, perhaps dropped completely, given the information about the late governor.

"We can't thank you enough," Zarant said, his hand on Cinch's shoulder. "For everything."

Cinch shrugged.

"And for that little going-away present to the *majivu,* I'm sure they can't thank you enough, either," O'thea said.

Cinch kept a deadpan expression. "A little bag I found in the woods," he said. "Dropped by a careless hiker or something. How valuable could it be?"

"The *majivu* will put it to good use, Cinch," she said.

"What abut you?" Zarant asked.

"Me? I'm going back to HQ, to fill out my report."

"After that, I mean?"

He shrugged again. "I don't know. I think maybe I'm getting too old for rangering. There's a woman on Roget I'd like to look up. Maybe she would enjoy a visit here."

"Maybe she would like it permanently?"

Cinch gave them a small grin. "It's a thought."

"Whatever you do, keep in touch, okay?"

He let the grin grow as he looked at her. "I will."

He climbed into the transport and nodded at the driver. The van pulled away into the hot afternoon. He was going to make his report and take a vacation. He had a lot to think about but he was pretty sure he would get it all sorted out.

Before he came home.

# AVONOVA PRESENTS
# AWARD-WINNING NOVELS
# FROM MASTERS OF SCIENCE FICTION